Elsie's Stolen Heart

Elsie's Stolen Heart

BOOK FOUR

of the
A Life of Faith:
Elsie Dinsmore
Series

Based on the beloved books by
Martha Finley

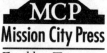

Mission City Press
Franklin, Tennessee

Book Four of the *A Life of Faith: Elsie Dinsmore* Series

Elsie's Stolen Heart
Copyright © 1999, Mission City Press, Inc.
All Rights Reserved.

Published by Mission City Press, Inc.

This series is based on the bestselling *Elsie Dinsmore* novels written by Martha Finley and first published in 1868 by Dodd, Mead & Company.

Cover & Interior Design: Richmond & Williams, Nashville, Tennessee
Cover Photography: Michelle Grisco Photography, West Covina, California
Typesetting: BookSetters, White House, Tennessee

Unless otherwise indicated, all Scripture references are from the Holy Bible New International Version (NIV). Copyright © 1973, 1978, 1984 by International Bible Society. Used by permission of Zondervan Publishing House, Grand Rapids, MI. All rights reserved.

Elsie Dinsmore and *A Life of Faith* are trademarks of Mission City Press, Inc.

For more information, write to Mission City Press 202 Second Avenue South, Franklin, Tennessee 37064, or visit our Web Site at **www.alifeoffaith.com**.

For a FREE catalog call 1-800-840-2641.

Library of Congress Catalog Card Number: 99-65157
Finley, Martha
       Elsie's Stolen Heart
       Book Four of the *A Life of Faith: Elsie Dinsmore* Series
       Hardcover: ISBN–10: 1-928749-04-6
                       ISBN–13: 978-1-928749-04-2
       Softcover: ISBN–10: 1-928749-83-6
                       ISBN–13: 978-1-928749-83-7

Printed in the United States of America
     7 8 9 10 11 — 11 10 09 08 07 06

DEDICATION

This book is
dedicated to
the memory of
MARTHA FINLEY

*May the rich legacy of
pure and simple devotion to Christ
that she introduced through
Elsie Dinsmore in 1868
live on in our day and
in generations to come.*

— FOREWORD —

*E*lsie Dinsmore is growing up. The lonely little heiress introduced in *Elsie's Endless Wait* is now a beautiful young woman of eighteen, on the verge of achieving the privileges and accepting the responsibilities of adulthood. But in the 1800s — just as today — the teenage years were a time when mistakes could be made that would alter the entire course of a person's life.

Martha Finley, the author of the original twenty-eight *Elsie* novels, wanted her books to be more than entertainment for her millions of readers. She hoped that her charming heroine would be "a pleasant companion and friend" and "a useful example" especially for young people "treading the same portion of life's pathway...." What is truly remarkable is that Elsie's stories continue to offer meaningful, Christ-centered guidance for young people and their parents almost a century and a half after they were written.

Elsie's Stolen Heart is the fourth in the *Elsie Dinsmore: A Life of Faith* series, carefully adapted from Miss Finley's novels. The first three books of the series follow Elsie's long struggle to win the love of her father without abandoning her Christian principles, the expansion of her family circle to include a new Mamma and a little brother, and Elsie's first marriage proposal.

In *Elsie's Stolen Heart*, she must face choices that put her loving and innocent nature to the gravest test she has yet faced. A number of new people enter her life, including her delightful great-aunt Wealthy Stanhope and the citizens of the small Ohio town of Lansdale. And a new kind of love captures her heart, but is it true or false? As Elsie experiences her first summer of independence, away from her father's tender protection, she will learn many lessons and confront complex feelings that challenge her ideals of love and loyalty, courtesy and obedience.

Mission City Press's goal in bringing these revised and adapted versions of the *Elsie* stories to contemporary readers is to assure that Martha Finley's vision of Christian living remains as vivid and relevant as it was in the author's era. Fashions and fads change over the years, but Elsie's life demonstrates that fundamental values are timeless. While Elsie and her creator would be astonished by the instant communication of television and computers and rapid travel by jet and automobile, they would feel comfortably at home with issues of the human heart and God's abiding love.

Elsie's Stolen Heart is an exciting and riveting tale from the past with a powerful message for young people and families confronting complicated problems and life-altering choices today. Martha Finley lit a candle of truth and hope in her time; Mission City Press is pleased to keep the flame burning brightly in ours.

❧ MANNERS & COURTSHIP IN ❧ ELSIE'S WORLD

When Elsie Dinsmore addresses her elders by their courtesy titles (Mr., Mrs., or Miss) and when she doesn't

interrupt adult conversations, she is using good manners. Manners are rules of behavior that affect the way people of all ages act toward one another. They are social rules that are outward signs of a society's values at a particular time. Although they aren't the same as laws or moral and religious codes, manners are important because they enable people to go about their day-to-day activities without too much misunderstanding and conflict.

In Elsie's day, the basic rules of mannerly behavior were similar in all parts of the United States: for example, children in Massachusetts and children in North Carolina were taught to show respect for adults, be kind to the less fortunate, and behave properly at meals and social gatherings.

But in the Old South in the colonial and Revolutionary eras, manners also played an important role in maintaining the social structure. Standards of behavior were often set by the wealthy class — the plantation families of Virginia and Maryland, the Carolinas, and Georgia who regarded themselves as "aristocrats." The rules then passed on to the middle class and the poor. Colonial Southerners based their code of manners on the etiquette of the English and European upper classes, and English books on manners such as *The Compleat Gentleman* and *The Whole Duty of Man* were commonly found in the libraries of the early plantation owners.

When wealthy and prominent Southern families such as the Dinsmores and the Carringtons got together, their manners tended to be formal; when the planters interacted with non-slaveholding, or "plain" farmers, merchants, tradespeople, and the like, their manners were more casual. But upper class Southerners generally believed in

the French concept of "noblesse oblige" — the obligation of the privileged to be thoughtful to people at every level of society. Good manners allowed people of different social status to mingle and conduct business without violating the class structure.

The Old South was rural and agricultural. There were few large cities, and people often had to travel long distances through sparsely populated forests and farmlands where there were no inns or resting places. So hospitality was highly valued. Rich and poor alike were expected to welcome traveling strangers into their homes, feeding them and providing shelter without expectation of payment. This "open door" neighborliness persisted until just before the Civil War. Even today, Southerners are regarded by their fellow Americans and foreign visitors as especially friendly — a reminder of the old tradition of welcoming strangers.

Another Southern tradition was honoring one's elders. Older people were shown special courtesy at all times by children and adults. In her autobiography, Mary Alves Long, who was born in North Carolina in the last year of the Civil War, recalled her childhood visits to her grandmother's. "It was understood that when you went to Grandma's you must always 'ask first,' even if it was only to pick up an apple from the apple-strewn ground under the May apple tree." Getting permission showed respect and good manners. [1]

Children were always expected to address older people by their courtesy titles and last names (Mr. Travilla, Doctor Barton), although relatives were spoken to by familiar names and titles (Mamma and Papa, Grandpa Dinsmore, Auntie Adelaide, etc.). Adults also used courtesy titles

Foreword

among themselves, and Southerners were famous for bestowing titles that weren't really deserved: a powerful man in a community might be addressed as "Colonel" or "Major" even though he never served in the military. When speaking to a child or adolescent not in their family, adults often used the courtesy titles "Miss" and "Master" with the child's first name, so Elsie is called "Miss Elsie" by acquaintances of the Dinsmores. Well-mannered children always said "yes, ma'am" and "no, sir" instead of a simple "yes" or "no."

Unfortunately, white Southerners did not apply to their slaves the rules they followed among themselves. Slaves and even free black people were not allowed courtesy titles, although house servants who were particularly close to the planter's family might be given the honorary titles of "Aunt" and "Uncle." But slaves were generally addressed by their first names only, and adult slaves might be called "boy" or "girl" by masters and other whites — cruel and arrogant habits that were calculated to reinforce the slave's low status.

Slaves adapted traditions from their African heritage to their situation in America, developing rules for behavior between one another and another set of rules for dealing with the slave owners and other white people. This second set of manners was designed to protect the slave from abuse. As an example of these two codes of behavior, among the slaves respect for and obligation to older people was very strong and genuine. But when a slave averted his eyes or bowed his head when speaking to a master or plantation overseer, it was an act of self-protection rather than respect.

The teaching of good manners began in the family but was carried on by church and school. The Ten Commandments

and other Scriptural injunctions instilled good manners as well as godly behavior. Proverbs and sayings like those from Benjamin Franklin's *Poor Richard's* almanacs and spiritual tales such as *Pilgrim's Progress* were often repeated in the nursery. Hodding Carter, a famous Southern journalist, remembered an elderly relative who lived in his childhood home and spoke "almost entirely in Biblical or secular proverbs, and they frequently were effective. Even now," Carter wrote when he was himself a grown man, "I can reel off scores of them. *Enough is as good as a feast. Children should be seen and not heard. Man shall not live by bread alone. Penny wise and pound foolish. Procrastination is the thief of time. Man proposes but God disposes. Fools rush in where angels fear to tread. Satan finds some mischief for idle hands to do. A stitch in time saves nine. As the twig is bent so is the tree inclined. The Lord loveth a cheerful giver. He who laughs last laughs best. Waste not, want not. Cut your garment according to your cloth....*" [2]

If all else failed, children who had a hard time learning their manners might be scared by superstitions such as the belief that a young man who takes the last food on the plate will never marry or that eating and singing at the same time brings bad luck. Belief in ghosts was common, and the fear of being "haunted" (a threat used to frighten Walter and little Enna Dinsmore into lying in *Elsie's Endless Wait*) prompted many a child to be on their best behavior.

≪ CHIVALRY AND COURTSHIP ≫

There were very few true aristocrats — people descended from the high-born and royal families of England and Europe — among the early Southerners.

Foreword

Money and political power separated the settlers into distinct social classes, and people who acquired wealth soon adopted fine manners to set themselves apart. In the beginning, they copied the manners and life styles of English country gentlemen, but from the 1820s to the Civil War, their role models were increasingly drawn from medieval history, poetry, and popular fictions about kings, knights, and damsels in distress.

The novels of Sir Walter Scott (1771-1832) were especially influential, and Southerners were attracted to romantic ideals of chivalry as presented in Scott's novels including *Ivanhoe*, *Kenilworth*, and *The Talisman*. The South was expanding rapidly westward, and the genteel and gentlemanly manners of the old Atlantic coast states did not work so well at the frontier and on the new cotton plantations that grew up from Alabama and Mississippi to Texas. In this rough and tumble environment, chivalrous manners and moral obligations appealed to people who had often risen from humble origins. Chivalry also helped maintain law and order by imposing a set of social expectations on the Southerner's instinctive sense of independence and freedom of action.

Chivalric ideals were gleaned by the relatively small number of educated Southerners from reading Scott and his imitators, the English Cavalier poets, and the legends of King Arthur and the Round Table. These ideas were quickly passed on to people at all levels and became part of the "Old South" mythology that flourished well into the 20th century.

Chivalry emphasized the ideals of Virtue, Honor, and Gallantry. The Southern gentleman, whether he came from the old "aristocracy" or the new wealthy class of the

west, was taught to put these ideals into practice by being loyal to family and honoring family ties, by protecting the weak and defenseless, and especially by respecting and defending the virtue and purity of women.

Few people lived up to the ideals of chivalry, and most people who were busy opening new territories, establishing farms, building roads, and raising towns didn't bother to try. But the ideals tended to set a tone that supported moral and religious teachings. A moral and mannerly man was never to swear or use profane language, drink to excess, gamble, cheat or lie, be cruel to people of lower rank, or behave in a cowardly manner. Most important, he was to treat women as ladies. A lady is by definition a woman; in the old use of the word, however, a "lady" is a woman of refinement and grace who, like Lady Rowena in *Ivanhoe*, deserves the courtly devotion and protection of knights and princes.

Although many historians agree that Southern women, both white and black, often worked harder, longer, and for fewer rewards than their menfolk, the image of the graceful and leisurely "lady of the manor" was powerful, especially in relation to the manners of courtship and marriage.

In colonial America, marriages among the wealthy were arranged by families who put material considerations above romance. By Elsie's time, however, romantic love was usually the deciding factor in choosing a marriage partner. Young women and men looked for people of "character" with whom to share their lives — wives who would be good-natured and loving, husbands who would be kind and dependable.

It was not unusual for women to marry as young as fifteen or sixteen and to choose men many years older. A gap

of ten or even twenty years between the ages of husband and wife was perfectly acceptable. The practical reason for this age difference was that women had few opportunities for higher education or independent careers. Women who did work, as teachers for example, were expected to give up their jobs when they married. Unless a young woman had an independent income or remained with her parents, marriage was the only avenue for economic security. So young women tended to seek their marriage partners among men who were already established as property owners or in business and could provide for a wife and family.

Because Southern communities were often isolated and travel was limited, people also tended to marry within their narrow social group. Even in modern times, visitors to rural southern towns often find that one or two family names are predominant and everyone in the community seems related by blood or marriage: the mayor is first cousin twice-removed of the elementary school principal who is great aunt of the high school football coach whose brother-in-law heads the local Chamber of Commerce and so on. This pattern of extended family relationships goes back to colonial and antebellum times. When Southerners spoke of "family pride," they meant loyalty not only to their immediate family but to distant relatives and connections through marriage as well.

Marriage was so important to families and communities that a good deal of energy was expended to get couples together. Events such as parties and dances, church meetings, picnics, barbecues and other social outings provided opportunities for unmarried men and women to meet under the ever-watchful eyes of parents and other adult chaperones. In the upper levels of society, particularly in major

cities such as New Orleans, Atlanta, and Charleston, young women might be presented to fashionable society when they reached marriageable age. "Coming out" balls and parties were a kind of announcement that a girl was available for courtship and marriage. In smaller communities, a girl's availability could be signaled in more casual ways: in Elsie's world, a change in hair style from childish curls to swept-up dos or dressing in more sophisticated fashions alerted potential suitors that a girl had become a young lady.

When a man wished to court a young woman, he called on her at her home; courting couples did not date or go out on their own. They were not often left by themselves, but even in privacy, the strictest standards of chivalry and propriety were maintained. Love letters could be exchanged between couples, and mild flirtation was permitted, but physical contact was minimal. A young woman's virtue was a matter of family pride and honor, and a man who attempted an unwanted kiss or embrace might well find himself challenged to a duel by angry brothers or uncles.

When a couple agreed to marry, it was customary to seek the consent of her father before announcing the engagement. In Elsie's time, families did not have absolute control over their daughters' and sons' marriage choices, but they exerted considerable influence. Marrying against family wishes might cause life-long rifts between family members, cutting a couple off from their strongest social ties and links to their community. So it is understandable that a man who had found his true love spent a great deal of his time proving his worth to her parents and family.

For a girl, the decision to marry was the single most important one of her life. Under the chivalric ideal,

women were seen as weak and fragile beings to be protected and supported first by their fathers and then by their husbands. In reality, this meant that women had very little control over the course of their lives after marriage. The real-life "Southern belle" — a character made popular in 20th century fiction and films about the pre-Civil War South such as Margaret Mitchell's *Gone With The Wind* — was often a young woman who used flirtation and frivolity to prolong the courtship period and delay marriage, knowing that she would lose virtually all freedom of choice at the marriage altar.

Under the laws of the time, a married woman was "inferior" to her husband, with few legal rights. Husbands legally controlled joint property and the treatment of children. Divorce was extremely difficult and uncommon in the Old South, and wives were expected to be submissive in all matters as long as the husband provided for his family. So a young woman who chose her husband unwisely could doom herself to a life of unrelieved misery.

Much of a young girl's education in manners and appropriate behavior was designed to help her make a happy marriage decision and become a successful wife and mother. When her mother and her aunts repeated the old saying "marry in haste, repent at leisure," they were teaching a lesson for life.

---

1. Mary Alves Long's autobiography, *High Time to Tell It*, was published by Duke University Press in 1950.

2. Hodding Carter is quoted from *Southern Legacy*, published by the Louisiana State University Press in 1950.

DINSMORE FAMILY TREE

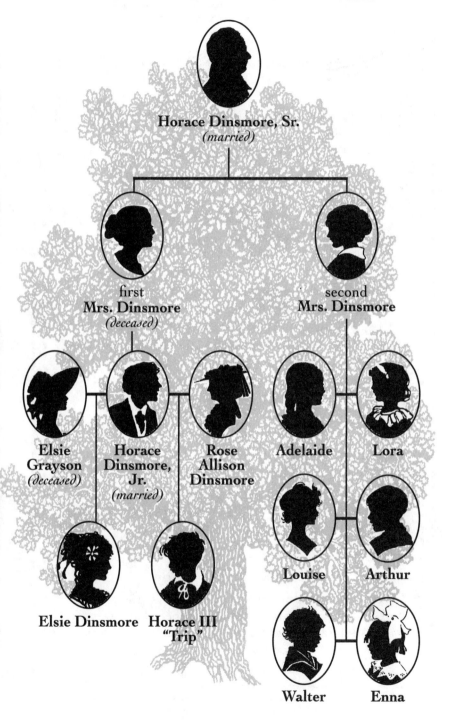

Horace Dinsmore, Sr.
(married)

first
Mrs. Dinsmore
(deceased)

second
Mrs. Dinsmore

Elsie Grayson
(deceased)

Horace Dinsmore, Jr.
(married)

Rose Allison Dinsmore

Adelaide

Lora

Elsie Dinsmore

Horace III "Trip"

Louise

Arthur

Walter

Enna

SETTING

$\mathcal{T}$he story begins in the early 1850s at The Oaks, the Old South plantation home of Horace Dinsmore, Jr., and his family.

CHARACTERS

∽ The Oaks ∽

Mr. Horace Dinsmore, Jr. — The only son of Horace Dinsmore, Sr., and father of Elsie Dinsmore. Horace is now remarried.

Rose Allison Dinsmore — Horace's second wife and beloved stepmother of Elsie.

Elsie Dinsmore — The only child of Horace Dinsmore, Jr., and Elsie Grayson, who died shortly after Elsie's birth. Elsie is now 18 years old.

Horace Dinsmore, III ("Trip") — Five-year-old son of Horace and Rose.

∽ Slaves of The Oaks ∽

Aunt Chloe — The middle-aged nursemaid who has cared for Elsie since birth and taught her in the Christian faith.

Jim — The stable manager who is often responsible for Elsie's safety.

John — Horace Dinsmore, Jr.'s personal servant.

∽ Roselands Plantation ∽

Mr. and Mrs. Horace Dinsmore, Sr. — Elsie's grandfather and his second wife. Their daughters are **Adelaide, Lora, Louise,** and **Enna**. Their sons **Arthur** and **Walter** are now attending college in the North.

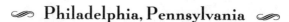

✍ Philadelphia, Pennsylvania ✍

Mr. and Mrs. Allison — A wealthy merchant and his wife who are the parents of **Rose Dinsmore**. Their other children are **Edward, Richard, Daniel, Sophie, Freddie, May**, and **Daisy**.

✍ Lansdale, Ohio ✍

Wealthy Stanhope — Horace Dinsmore, Jr.'s elderly aunt.

Phyllis and Simon — Miss Stanhope's servants.

Dr. and Mrs. King — Miss Stanhope's next-door neighbors who have two daughters, **Lottie** and **Nettie**.

Mrs. Nickle — Another neighbor, she has two children: **Lenwilla Ellawea** ("Willy") and **Corbinus** ("Binny")

✍ Others ✍

Edward Travilla — Owner of Ion Plantation and closest friend of Horace Dinsmore, Jr.

Mr. and Mrs. Carrington and their daughter **Lucy** — Old friends of the Dinsmores, they live at Ashlands Plantation.

Tom Jackson ("Bromly Edgerton") — A new acquaintance of Arthur Dinsmore.

Mr. and Mrs. Beresford and their son **Rudolph** — Residents of Cincinnati, they are good friends of Edward Travilla.

CHAPTER

1

An Invitation to Visit

"Ask and it will be given to you;
seek and you will find;
knock and the door
will be opened to you."

MATTHEW 7:7

*A*t The Oaks, it had been a particularly warm and wet spring, and Horace and Rose Dinsmore were hoping to begin their holiday a bit early to escape the coming heat. It was the custom for wealthy landowners to take their families to cooler climes in summer, away from the fever epidemics that so often swept the plantations of the South. Some chose the mountains for their seasonal retreats, but the Dinsmores preferred the ocean and for several years had taken a summer house in a New Jersey seaside community. They were discussing their plans at the breakfast table one morning.

Closing her delicately carved sandalwood fan, Rose asked, "Do you think we can get the cottage this soon in the year?"

"I doubt it will be a problem," Horace replied. "I wrote to my agent two weeks ago, and I'm certain he can make all the necessary arrangements. I expect to hear from him any day now."

"We've already begun the packing," his wife said. "I really don't think we would be half so well prepared if it weren't for Elsie and Aunt Chloe." Rose smiled across the table at her step-daughter — the loving child who had always been so dear to her and who was now becoming a beautiful young woman.

Elsie looked back with a happy expression. "It's mostly Aunt Chloe's doing," she said of her nursemaid. "I believe she is the most efficient woman in the world."

"She's kept us organized for more years than I care to remember," Horace said. "Why Elsie, do you realize that it was almost ten years ago that I first beheld you? I shall always regret that I missed so much of your childhood, but we have traveled many interesting roads since then, have we not?"

Before Elsie could reply, a chipper little voice asked, "And how many years since you first *beheld* me, Papa?"

"Well, let's see, Son. How old are you?"

The bright-cheeked little boy laughed. "Don't you know that, Papa? I'm five, Papa. I was born five years ago."

"And since I first saw you not very many minutes after you were born . . . "

"You *beheld* me five years ago!" Trip exclaimed. Then his expression turned earnest, and he began slowly to count with his fingers. Trip was the third "Horace Dinsmore" in the family, named for his father and grandfather; his nickname "Trip" was bestowed by his big sister, Elsie, because his name was a triple. Now, like his sister, he was being schooled by his father and mother. A bright and inquisitive child, he had quickly taken to his arithmetic lessons and enjoyed doing simple sums. After a few moments of concentration, he proclaimed, "Papa! Since I am five, and Elsie is almost eighteen now — then she was almost thirteen when she *beheld* me!"

Everyone laughed, and Horace said, "That's right, Trip. Very well done."

"And what a sight you were," Elsie teased. "A bright red face and big eyes and not a hair on your head."

Instinctively Trip patted at his thick, dark brown curls. "No hair at all?" he asked in amazement.

"Hardly a one," his mother said sweetly, "but you were a very handsome baby nonetheless."

An Invitation to Visit

"And you are still the handsomest brother I could want," Elsie added with a gentle smile. Trip's grin spread across his face, and for a moment Elsie was struck with a sense of wonder at this family of hers. When she was Trip's age, she had been alone and lonely — an outcast in her grandfather's home with only her nursemaid to care for her and the love of God to sustain her. Then her father had returned to claim her, and he had married Rose, who was everything a motherless child could hope for. Little Trip had added untold joy to their lives. A quick prayer of thanksgiving passed through Elsie's mind: "Thank you, Lord, for Your boundless goodness to me and my family."

It was at that moment that Jim, the servant who managed the stables and horses, entered. He was carrying a bulging canvas bag which he presented to Horace.

"Thank you, Jim," Horace said. "It seems we have an abundance of mail today."

"Yes, sir. And there's a couple of newspapers and a package for Miss Elsie, too."

"I hope it's my book," Elsie said.

Horace began removing the contents from the bag and distributing the letters around the table. There were several for Rose, and one for little Trip from his grandmother in Philadelphia. The excited little boy rushed to his mother's side to have his letter read; Elsie unwrapped her package, which was indeed a new book, and Horace looked through the remaining letters. Extracting a cream-colored envelope from the stack, he said, "Now here is a handwriting that I have not seen in some time."

"Who is it from, dear?" Rose asked.

"Have I ever told you about my Aunt Wealthy Stanhope?" he responded as he opened the envelope and took out several pages of stiff notepaper.

"Who?" Rose said.

"An aunt we have never heard of?" Elsie added with some surprise. "Who is she, Papa?"

"You know that my mother was a Stanhope," Horace began. "Well, my grandfather Stanhope was married twice, and Aunt Wealthy is the daughter of his first wife, who died. My mother was the daughter of his second wife, so she and Aunt Wealthy were half-sisters. Aunt Wealthy was some eight or ten years older than my mother, so she would be in her seventies now. She never married and always refused to live with any of her relations. She resides quite happily in her own home in Ohio."

"Did you know her, Papa?" Elsie inquired. Her interest was roused by this news of a previously unknown relative.

"When I was small, my mother spoke of her, but I met Aunt Wealthy only once — about the time you were born, Elsie. I am afraid I was in no state of mind then to appreciate her. When I was eighteen, I regarded her as a fussy old maid of no concern to me. In fact, I believe her to be a good and noble little woman, though decidedly odd in some respects."

"And this letter is from her?" Rose inquired.

"Yes," Horace said, bending his head to the pages and quickly reading the contents.

"This is interesting," he said at last, raising his eyes to Elsie. "She has invited Elsie and me to pay her a visit. And she would like Elsie to stay with her for the summer."

An Invitation to Visit

"In Ohio?" Elsie asked, her curiosity now mingling with a little trepidation, for she had not been parted from her father for so long a time or over such a distance in many years.

"Lansdale, Ohio," Horace said. "It is a very pleasant town, I think, and not too far from Cincinnati. What do you say to a visit there, Elsie dear?"

"I should like to visit if you go, Papa. But the entire summer?"

Passing the letter to his daughter, Horace said, "Read for yourself. If we accept Aunt Wealthy's invitation to visit, I don't think you need decide on staying for the summer until we go there."

Elsie read the letter, which was written in an old-fashioned, spidery script. In it, Aunt Wealthy described her village as a pretty and healthful place blessed with lovely scenery and polite society. Briefly she told about her own home, which she said offered more than enough room for her great-niece's comfort. And she happily mentioned her next-door neighbors whose household included two lively young women of about Elsie's age who would make excellent companions.

As Elsie perused the letter, Rose inquired of her husband, "What did you mean when you said that your aunt is 'odd in some respects'?"

Horace laughed. "Be assured, dearest, that she is proper in every way and would make an excellent guardian for Elsie. But Aunt Wealthy has her own manner of doing things. Her dress and hair style, for instance, are all her own, unless she has decided to follow the fashions since I last saw her. And she has a peculiar habit of speech."

At Rose's startled look, he explained, "Aunt Wealthy has a way of transposing sentences that is quite unique. And she tends to speak of people not by their names but by words she associates with the real names. Miss Bell, for instance, she would probably call Miss Ring. Mr. Foot would be Mr. Shoe, and so on."

"That's funny, Papa," Trip giggled. "What do you think she would call me?"

"Well, Son, we call you Trip, so your Aunt Wealthy might introduce you as Stumble."

"But it is not an intentional habit?" Elsie queried.

"Not at all. Her mistakes are always innocent and very charming."

Elsie read the letter a second time and found it, too, to be a charming invitation. She had become more curious than ever about this Wealthy Stanhope — in part because of her father's description, but also because the news of a new great-aunt intrigued her. Except for her Grandpa Horace's family, she had never known any other living relatives.

As it happened, the morning's mail included an invitation from Rose's parents in Philadelphia. Mr. and Mrs. Allison longed to see their eldest daughter and her family. Their letter urged Rose and Horace to bring Elsie and Trip for a visit before their summer retreat on Cape May.

Horace's agent had also written to say that rental of the Cape cottage could begin as early as the second week of June.

"Well," Horace said with satisfaction, "it seems that all the pieces have fallen in place. We shall journey together to Philadelphia, and after several days there, Elsie and I can continue on to Aunt Wealthy's home in Ohio. If Elsie decides to stay with Aunt Wealthy, as I believe she well might, then I shall return to Philadelphia, collect Rose and Trip, and proceed on to the Cape house. If you choose to accompany us, Elsie, that will be fine, too. At any rate, Elsie and I will have our little family reunion in Ohio, and the Allisons will be able to spoil Trip for a week or two. How does that sound?"

As Elsie and Rose both nodded assent, little Trip ran to his father's side. His bright eyes round with questioning, he demanded, "How will Grandpa and Grandma Allison spoil me, Papa? Will they spoil me like milk spoils?"

"They will spoil you with love and affection, Son," Horace laughed, "and you will enjoy every minute with them."

Three weeks later, in a large, well-kept house on the outskirts of Lansdale, Ohio, a sweet voice that reminded some people of a bird's song called out, "Phyllis! Simon! Are you two up yet? It's nearly five o'clock, and the train will be arriving at six."

A boy of about fifteen poked his head over the railing of the back staircase. "Coming, Miss Wealthy," he said and hurriedly descended the stairs into the spotless kitchen. "Don't you worry, ma'am. I've got plenty of time to do all my chores and get to the depot before your kinfolk arrive."

He was followed closely by a middle-aged woman who was still buttoning the strap of her apron as she came down the stairs.

"Whew, Miss Wealthy," the woman said, "I didn't expect you to be up before me. But here you are, all dressed and looking so nice, and the sun's hardly shown his face over the treetops yet."

"Phyllis, you know that I always wake early when something is about to occur," said the little lady. She turned to the boy and commanded, "Hurry on and feed the horses, Simon. I want you to have old Joan hitched to the carriage and waiting at the front gate at a quarter to six sharp. Now, did you arrange with Mr. Laugh for the one-horse cart? We need that for their luggage."

"I arranged it with Mr. *Grinn*," Simon replied with a smile. "I'll have Old Joan and the carriage at the gate, and I'll follow on behind with Mr. Grinn's cart."

"Very well, then. I showed you the pictures of my nephew and his daughter and their servant woman yesterday. Will you recognize them?"

"I surely will," Simon said as he hastened out the kitchen door.

"Now, we must hurry, too," Aunt Wealthy said to Phyllis, her nursemaid and cook for many years and mother of young Simon. "We want to have a breakfast ready this morning that's fit for a king! Can you have it on the table when they arrive from the train?"

"I can, Miss Wealthy, but let's give your folks a few minutes to wash up and settle 'fore we set them down to eat."

"Ah, yes, that's right. Then can you have breakfast ready by seven o'clock?"

"If I could feed 'em at six, I can feed 'em at seven," the nursemaid chuckled, "so long as you let me get to my work."

Aunt Wealthy turned and left the kitchen, but a few seconds later she was back.

"Are their rooms ready?"

"Ready as they'll ever be," Phyllis said.

"And towels? Are the fresh towels laid out?"

"You know they are."

"The flower arrangements! Goodness, Phyllis, did we set them out?"

"Right before bed last night," the bemused maid replied to her anxious employer. "Miss Wealthy, I don't think I've seen you this excited in some time. Now you know there isn't a speck of dust left in this whole house after all our cleaning, and not a thing out of place. But if you want something to do, why not give that front porch one last sweep."

"That's a good idea," Wealthy agreed. Taking a broom from the pantry, she disappeared, and with a little sigh, Phyllis set about her cooking.

A little later, as Aunt Wealthy was furiously applying her broom to the porch steps, the front gate opened, and a smiling girl with roguish black eyes came up the gravel path. She was dressed in a simple brown linen suit, but her snowy white cuffs and collar set off her tan complexion and red cheeks. A small straw hat crowned her raven hair.

"Good morning, Aunt Wealthy!" the girl sang out. "You see, I am on time."

Stopping her sweeping, Aunt Wealthy looked the girl over. "And neat as a pin, too, dear Lottie" she said approvingly. "It's very kind of you to offer to introduce yourself and meet them at the depot because I want to meet them here, of course, as they come."

Aunt Wealthy's young next-door neighbor, who was used to the lady's sometimes strange speech, laughed. "It's no trouble at all. But you've told me that Mr. Dinsmore is a wealthy

man and his daughter is an heiress. Do you think they will turn up their aristocratic noses at someone like me?" she teased.

"Oh, I don't think they are of that sort," Aunt Wealthy said earnestly. "But if they should turn up their noses at you, Lottie, then you turn yours up at them."

Lottie laughed heartily. "I doubt that they are snobs at all. From the pictures you showed me, Miss Dinsmore looks very sweet and agreeable. Besides, they are your kin, so how could they be other than nice?" she said.

Wealthy was about to reply when they heard the creaking of the carriage and the plopping of Old Joan's hooves on the dry dirt street. As Simon guided the carriage to the gate, Wealthy said, "We shall see soon enough what they are like. Off you go, Lottie, and be careful."

CHAPTER

2

At Home in Ohio

*"The boundary lines have fallen
for me in pleasant places;
surely I have a delightful
inheritance."*

PSALM 16:6

At Home in Ohio

*L*ottie and Simon were as good as their word, arriving at the depot several minutes before the morning train pulled in. Simon was the first to spot Horace, Elsie, and Aunt Chloe as they alighted from the train. Introductions were made, and Lottie, politely refusing Horace's offer to drive the carriage, was soon leading their small caravan through Lansdale, past neat stores and pretty houses that were unlike any Elsie had seen before.

Not many minutes passed before Lottie pulled up the reins and brought Old Joan to a halt in front of a tasteful, two-story dwelling built in the Gothic style. Masses of climbing roses, honeysuckle, and Virginia creeper spread over its walls, festooning the gables of the upper story and twining around the pillars of a broad front porch. The yard, separated from the street by a spiked iron fence, comprised neatly trimmed lawn bordered by lush, low-growing bushes and beds thick with bright spring flowers.

In the midst of this perfect picture stood a little woman in an outfit that defied all the rules. Her patterned chintz dress was ruffled at the neck (where Fashion dictated plainness) and had a slim, gored skirt (where Fashion demanded fullness). The skirt in fact stopped just above the wearer's ankles, revealing the white stockings and small black slippers beneath (shocking to Fashion). The little woman wore her gray hair done into a knot almost on top of her head with two thick curls held by combs at the sides of her face. (Fashion frowned.)

As Horace handed Elsie from the carriage, Aunt Wealthy rushed to greet them at the gate. Taking Horace's hand, she smiled broadly and said, "I'm so glad you've come, nephew. So very glad."

Horace bent to kiss her cheek; then Aunt Wealthy turned to embrace Elsie. "I didn't expect you, dear," Wealthy said.

At Elsie's startled look, Wealthy quickly went on, "I mean, of course, that I expected you to be here, but I didn't expect you to be so beautiful and grown-up. Your picture didn't do you justice. Come now, come inside. You too, dear," she added, beckoning to Lottie. "Simon, leave the horses for a spell and take Miss Dinsmore's nursemaid and the luggage to meet Phyllis."

Inside, the house was cool and inviting. In the old-fashioned parlor, the guests chatted with their hostess for several minutes, until Simon reappeared to show Horace to his room. Lottie excused herself, promising to return later. And Wealthy guided Elsie upstairs to a plainly furnished bedroom that the girl, so used to the luxuries of The Oaks, judged to be charming in its simplicity. The brass bed and the dressing table were draped in crisp, white linens, and white muslin curtains billowed at the windows. Vases filled with fresh flowers decorated the mantel and dresser and filled the room with delicate fragrance. Curls of green vines peeped in at the casement windows, from which the room looked down upon the gardens and across to several houses behind which green fields rolled gently into broad, low hills.

"It's a lovely room. I shall be so comfortable here," Elsie exclaimed with genuine enthusiasm. Instinctively she took her great-aunt's tiny hand in hers and said, "You are so kind to invite Papa and me."

Aunt Wealthy's eyes shone with pleasure. "It is you and your father who are kind to visit, for I'd never visit you. Oh dear, I mean that I never travel much beyond Lansdale, and a journey to the South is beyond my endurance."

"I understand," Elsie assured, "for it is a long and tiring trip. But your home and this room offer a most welcome retreat."

"Indeed, child, that is my wish for you," Wealthy replied softly. Then she cocked her little head. "There," she said, "I hear your nursemaid on the stairs. Why don't you freshen up and then come down for breakfast in ten minutes or so."

When Chloe entered, introductions were made, and Wealthy hurried away to check that Horace had everything he required.

Chloe had brought one of Elsie's valises and began to unpack it. "That boy Simon will have the rest of your luggage up here soon," she said. "I'll put everything away while you're eating."

"But what about you, Aunt Chloe?" Elsie asked. "When will you eat?"

"Honey, I already ate, and let me tell you something. That Phyllis is some fine cook. Why, her buttered biscuits beat all. And bacon just as good as a Virginia ham. I sure am glad you've reached the age where your Papa lets you eat what you like now, 'cause you're gonna dine mighty well here."

Elsie laughed, "Yes, it's nice to have something more than stewed fruit and bread and milk in the morning. But I still follow Papa's rules, you know. I think Papa is right about watching what children eat."

"I think so, too, Miss Elsie. I believe that his being so careful about you is part of what got you back so healthy after you were so sick. That and the good Lord's love and protection. I didn't necessarily agree with Mr. Horace back then, but I do now. He and your Mamma Rose are mighty wise to be bringing up little Trip the same as you. And speaking of healthy, that Miss Stanhope is a spry little bird."

"You know that she's past seventy," Elsie said.

"I do, but she bustles around like a woman half her age. She's a bit odd in her dress, but that Phyllis says Miss Stanhope's 'bout the kindest lady she knows."

Chloe was right about the breakfast, and both Horace and Elsie ate well before retiring to their rooms for a rest. Elsie, who never understood how people could sleep on trains, napped till almost dinner time when Chloe woke her. Elsie quickly bathed, and Chloe was helping her into a clean summer frock when they heard a strange, high-pitched yelping sound. Rushing to the window, they were met by a comical sight below — a fat poodle had stuffed its plump body between the railings of the front gate and was stuck there, protesting loudly.

As they watched, Wealthy Stanhope rushed down the path to the dog, grabbed it firmly by the haunches, and yanked it free. Whimpering but apparently unharmed, the dog allowed itself to be petted and soothed. "Albert, you naughty thing," Wealthy was saying. "I didn't want to hurt you, but how else was I to get you out, or in. You must learn to stay at home."

Then the little woman, still holding on to Albert, looked up and called in her bird-like voice, "Thomas! Thomas! You get home, too!"

Across the street, Elsie and Chloe saw a large marmalade cat emerge from beneath a hydrangea bush and amble lazily toward his mistress.

"So those are Aunt Wealthy's pets," Elsie said. "Albert and Thomas — what odd names for a dog and a cat."

"Yes ma'am," Chloe agreed, "but Phyllis says that Miss Stanhope is mighty good to her pets and just about any animal that comes by."

Chloe had just put the finishing touches to Elsie's hair when they heard the dinner bell ring, followed by a gentle tapping at the door. It was Horace, looking much rested himself and ready to escort his daughter to the mid-day meal.

After another of Phyllis's excellent meals, Wealthy took her guests on a grand tour of her house. She led them to the parlor and showed them a number of items, some quite faded and worn but all of excellent quality, which had been in her family for generations.

"These may look like ancient relics to you children," Wealthy said, pointing out a frayed Oriental carpet and several pieces of mahogany furniture, "but I am old-fashioned. I treasure them all as part of our family history. See that sampler?" she said, indicating a framed wall hanging, intricately embroidered with the letters of the alphabet and a beautiful landscape. "That is a specimen of my father's grandmother's handiwork. She would be your great-great grandmother, Horace. She embroidered those cushions, too, and filled them with her own feathers, so I value them more than their weight in gold."

Horace politely remarked how much his sister Adelaide would enjoy seeing such lovely needlework. But Elsie, who was adjusting to Wealthy's strange speech, could not help smiling at the image of a great-great-grandmother who grew feathers.

After seeing the treasures of the parlor, sitting room, and library, the little group adjourned to the front porch. Wealthy supplied Horace with a newspaper and herself with a basket of knitting. Elsie had her new book, but was content to enjoy the lovely garden and chat quietly with her aunt. After some time, she noticed that Wealthy had nodded off over her work.

Waking with a start, Wealthy exclaimed, "Do forgive me! I rose quite early this morning and have been stirring ever since."

"Please, Aunt Wealthy," Elsie said, "you must take a nap. Papa has gone in to write some letters, and I have this book for company. You have earned some rest."

"I think I will lie down for a little while," Wealthy said, rising from her rocking chair. "I'll just be in the sitting room, dear, so please wake me if anyone comes to call."

Elsie had been reading for some time when a sharp, little voice broke into her thoughts.

"Who are you?" it said.

Looking up, Elsie found herself inches away from the freckled face of a little girl in a gingham sunbonnet.

"Who are you?" Elsie asked in return.

The little girl puffed out her chest and said importantly, "I am Lenwilla Ellawea Nickle. I bet you're the rich young lady from the South who's come to see Miss Wealthy."

Suppressing her smile, Elsie said, "I have come from the South to visit my great-aunt. Won't you be seated?"

Lenwilla Ellawea Nickle strode over to Wealthy's rocking chair and sat upon it as if it were a queen's throne.

"Where did you get such an imposing name?" Elsie asked.

"My Mamma made it up, and my brother's too. His name is Corbinus, but we call him Binny."

"And what are you called?"

"Willy."

"And do you live near here, Willy?"

"Just over yonder," the child said, pointing to a smallish house on the opposite side of the street. "My father's dead, but Mamma and Binny and me live there. Mamma will come to see you sometime."

"I'd like to meet her," Elsie replied.

At that, Willy popped up from the chair. Saying "I gotta go now," she was off the porch and dashing across the lawn before Elsie could manage another word.

Elsie watched the little girl cross the dusty street and disappear into a gate at a house across the way. "Strange and stranger," she said to herself with a smile.

"So you've met Willy," said Aunt Wealthy, who had awakened from her afternoon nap much refreshed. She had served her guests a delicious cold supper and was now treating Elsie and Horace to a tour of her garden. "She often stops by to borrow some little thing or other. The whole family always has something that they're out of."

"She?" Horace said in surprise. "This Willy is a she?"

"Yes, Papa, " Elsie said. "Willy is her nickname, and she lives just a little way down the street."

"The family is a little odd," said Wealthy in a confiding way. "I'm sure you will meet Mrs. Penny someday soon."

"But I thought she said their name is Nickle," Elsie said.

"Of course, it is Nickle and not Penny. I am always forgetting their exact value," Wealthy laughed, "and I am always apt to get names wrong rather than right."

"Well, little Willy's full name is a mouthful," Elsie explained to her father, who was understandably bewildered by this conversation. "It is Lenwilla Ellawea Nickle. Mrs. Nickle must have an unusual taste in names."

"She is a manufacturer of them, and very proud of her products," Wealthy agreed.

The gardens were a special source of pride and joy to Wealthy; she was a great lover of flowers and did much of the cultivation with her own hands. As she led her nephew and great-niece around the house, they saw that the beauty of the front garden extended to the rear where a great variety of beautiful blooms greeted their view. Further on they came to a chicken house where Phyllis was feeding a cackling army of fowl.

"You have quite a flock," Horace commented.

"I like to see them running around the yard," Wealthy said. "Besides, the eggs you lay yourself are so much better than the ones you buy, and the chickens have quite another taste."

Suddenly Wealthy changed her tone and commanded, "You there, Albert. Get away from those birds. And Thomas, come here now."

Reluctantly, the dog and the cat came away from the interesting activity in the chicken yard and ambled up to their mistress.

"You seem to have a good many pets, Auntie," Elsie remarked as they all walked back to the house.

"And I am very fond of them all," Wealthy replied as she scooped Thomas the cat into her arms. "Having no children, I have my pets to love. But I have another I love even more — my great-nephew Harry Duncan. He's away at school now, but I hope to show him to you one of these days."

"I'd like to see him," Elsie said. "Is he another member of our family?" she asked her father.

"No, the Duncans are on Aunt Wealthy's other side."

"Well, Thomas is a fine cat," Elsie said, gently stroking the purring animal in her great-aunt's arms, "and very handsome."

"I raised him, and his mother before him," Wealthy said. "My sister Beulah was the first husband's child of Harry's grandmother twice-married. Yes I think a great deal of him, but we came near to losing him last winter. A fellow in town — he's two years old now — got an idea to make a sleigh blanket of cat's fur, and he told the boys he'd pay ten cents for every cat skin they could bring him. Well, nobody's cat was safe then, and I had to keep him locked up so he wouldn't be turned into a rug."

Elsie listened to this story with growing perplexity. Who was Beulah? Did Aunt Wealthy mean she had raised the cat or the nephew? And which was two? Surely not the man who wanted the cat skin blanket. Elsie looked to her father, her confusion plain in her face, but Horace could only shrug his shoulders. He was as mystified as his daughter. He was about to question his aunt when footsteps and voices were heard from the porch, and the doorbell rang.

"It's Lottie and her father," Wealthy declared. She put Thomas down and welcomed her friends. "Come in, friends, and don't stand on ceremony."

Lottie was already through the door, followed by a smiling, gray-haired man in his middle years.

"Good evening," Lottie said gaily. "Mr. Dinsmore, I have brought my father, Dr. King, to meet you and Miss Dinsmore."

The two men shook hands, and Dr. King said jovially, "I thought Lottie should introduce me lest our dear Aunt Wealthy forget my nobility and present me, as she often does, to be a Prince rather than a King."

Wealthy laughed at this joke on herself. "It is a mistake I don't make as often now as I used to," she protested with good humor.

"Well, to make amends to you, Aunt Wealthy, I will admit to all that my wife says that you are the better doctor of us. She wanted me to tell you that the bran has worked wonders."

"Bran?" Horace asked.

"Yes, sir," Dr. King replied. "My wife was suffering from indigestion, and Miss Stanhope advised her to eat a tablespoon of bran after every meal."

"It is a remedy my father learned from an old sea-captain," Wealthy explained.

"Aunt Wealthy is no end of surprises," the doctor said to Horace and Elsie.

Later, after the Kings had gone and Wealthy had bid her nephew and great-niece good-night, Horace escorted Elsie to her room where they shared a Scripture reading and prayer.

"I believe we shall both sleep soundly this night," he said, suppressing a yawn. "Tell me, dear, what are your impressions of your great-aunt and her home?"

"Well, Papa," Elsie said thoughtfully. "She is good and kind and unlike any woman I have ever met. She is a bit odd, to be sure, but in the sweetest way. She doesn't live lavishly, yet this house feels like a retreat from care. I haven't quite decided if I should stay for the summer, but I'm awfully glad we've come to Lansdale."

"I, too, dear Daughter," said Horace as he opened the door to leave. "And if you do chose to stay, I will know that you will be in the safest of hands."

CHAPTER

3

Hatching
A Plot

"This only have I found:
God made mankind upright,
but men have gone in search
of many schemes."

ECCLESIASTES 7:29

*A*t the very moment Horace Dinsmore and his daughter were discussing their first day in Lansdale, two young college men were having an altogether different discussion some five hundred miles to the east.

"You can't be going out, Art. It's after ten o'clock, and you know the college rules," Walter Dinsmore was saying.

"It's none of your business when I go out," Arthur replied with irritation. "We share these rooms, my brother. But you are not my keeper."

"No, I'm not your keeper," Walter sighed, "but I can remind you of the promises you made to our father. Are you gambling again?"

Arthur slammed his fist down on his brother's desk, rattling the ink well and pens and causing a book to tumble to the floor.

"How I keep my promises is not your problem!" he shouted. "Now go back to your studies, little brother, and tend to your own concerns."

His face dark with emotion, Arthur grabbed his hat and jacket and stormed out of the small apartment. Walter listened to his brother's heavy steps on the stairs, followed by the closing of the front door of their dormitory building. He put his head in his hands and rubbed his eyes. "I'm sure he's gambling again," Walter muttered to himself, "but what can I do about it? I could report him to Papa or the school, but Arthur would never forgive me for telling tales behind his back. Oh, maybe I'm wrong. Maybe he just wants to go out for some fresh air."

Walter leaned down and retrieved his book from the floor. He still had an hour of study to complete before he could go to sleep. "You just worry about your duties, and let Arthur tend to his," he said to himself, and his words sounded hollowly in the room.

⚬⚬⚬

Careful not to be observed, Arthur stole out of the college grounds and made his way to an area of the city where few decent people ever found themselves at this time of night. As he approached a corner lighted by a street lamp, a figure emerged from the shadows.

"You're late, Dinsmore," the man said.

"I had to escape my brother's eagle eyes," Arthur replied angrily. "He is worse than an old nursemaid."

"Cheer up, my boy," the man said, clapping Arthur's bent shoulders. "Your day of emancipation comes soon, doesn't it? When will you be twenty-one?"

"Next year. But little good it will do me. Unlike my older brother, I will have nothing of my own until one or the other of my respected parents sees fit to kick the bucket and leave me a bundle. And neither seems inclined to do so any time soon."

"Then you must take your chances at the gambling tables," the man said and began to lead Arthur down the dark street.

"Chances?" Arthur replied. "What chances have I when you win everything I own, Jackson. If my luck doesn't begin to turn, I — I'll . . . "

Arthur's thought was unspoken, but Jackson could easily hear the bitterness in the younger man's tone. And bitterness, he knew, led to recklessness.

Hatching A Plot

"Bah!" Jackson laughed. "We all have our ups and downs, old man. You must take your turn at both, like the rest of us."

Not many more steps brought them to a darkened house. They ascended the stone stairs and knocked at the door. It was opened instantly by a waiter who ushered them immediately into a hallway lighted only by a single candle. Arthur and Jackson proceeded down the hall to a door that led into a brightly lit and grandly furnished room with heavy chairs and couches covered in plush velvet. The windows were covered over in thick, velvet draperies that kept the light from escaping. Along a wall, a table was spread with trays of rich foods, bottles of fine wines and crystal goblets, and boxes of cigars. The men went directly to the table where Jackson filled a plate for himself and Arthur took a glass of wine.

Jackson spent some time with his meal. He praised the fresh oysters and the delicate pastries, but Arthur only drank his wine and then got another glass of the potent liquid. At last Jackson went back to the table, taking a cigar for himself and refilling Arthur's glass.

The wine had calmed Arthur somewhat, but he was anxious to get on with the purpose of his visit, so the two men left the parlor and went up a flight of stairs to a second room — decorated like the first but filled with tables around which men of various ages sat playing card games. That they were gambling was immediately obvious from the piles of silver and gold coins and paper bank notes that lay before them.

"How about a game of Faro, old man?" Jackson asked, knowing full well that Arthur was addicted to this costly game of chance.

Elsie's Stolen Heart

Arthur immediately found his seat at a marble-topped table behind which a dealer stood. Jackson sat down beside him. Under the strong light in the room, it was clear that Arthur and his companion were handsome young men — Jackson especially so with his strong, dark features and sardonic smile. He was several years older than Arthur, and, as soon became obvious, the better card player. In fact, Jackson was a professional gambler, and Arthur was his current victim.

Jackson had spotted Arthur some weeks earlier. Sensing weakness, he had befriended the younger man and easily tempted him deeper and deeper into the world of vice. Tonight, Jackson assured himself, he would finish the job. He already held many of Arthur's IOUs. If the boy lost everything tonight, he would have to go to his rich, old father to cover the losses, and when he did, Jackson could walk away with a handsome profit for his efforts.

Indeed, Arthur was playing like a wild man, betting high and taking lunatic risks. Each game only made him more frenzied. Jackson (who had connived with the card dealer to cheat and so ran no danger of loss) allowed Arthur to win at first. Convinced that his "luck" had turned, Arthur doubled and trebled his bets. As he risked larger and larger amounts, Jackson reeled the gullible boy in with the skill of a fisherman landing a prize catch.

It did not take long. Less than an hour after he sat down at the gaming table, Arthur rose slowly from his chair. His face was a deathly pale, and he had to steady himself several times as he walked from the garish, smoke-filled room.

Hatching A Plot

Jackson followed him, saying nothing until they had left the building and reached the sidewalk. Then in a tone as smooth as butter, he consoled, "Bad luck, old man. But you can always win it back."

Arthur turned on his heel and demanded in a voice that cracked with emotion, "With what? I've lost it all to you, Tom. I'm thousands in the hole by now."

"True. And it is a debt of honor which I know you will pay. But you have the resources."

"Resources? I've told you what my resources are. Nothing! Unless my father drops dead in his tracks tonight, I have nothing! I'm ruined!"

"Surely not," Jackson said calmly. "Your father would never allow you to face a public scandal. If you write to him —"

"Never," Arthur said sullenly. Bowing his head, he began to move away, but Jackson was instantly at his side. They walked along the street for some minutes, until Arthur suddenly stopped. It was too dark for Jackson to see more than the outline of the younger man's face, but he could make out Arthur's posture, erect now with shoulders straight.

"Suppose I show you how to marry a fortune. Will you cancel my gambling debts?" Arthur asked.

"Depends on your scheme," the other man replied. "And the size of the fortune. I am not a marrying man."

"But you have quite a reputation as a lady-killer, and I know you to be quite skilled at the manipulation of weaker types," Arthur said, keeping his voice free of the bitterness that was twisting his heart. At this moment, Tom Jackson repulsed him, but Arthur was in the man's power and could not afford to show contempt.

"I — I have a plan," he continued. "It will take some time to bring off, but the results are well worth it, I assure you."

Jackson laughed. "If it is such a fortune, why would you hand it over to me? Who is the target? Not one of your sisters?"

Arthur's lips curled in scorn: "Hardly. But she is almost as close — my brother's daughter, eighteen, beautiful, and heiress to a large fortune."

"Ah," Jackson sighed. "You've said before that your brother is wealthy, but I believe he is healthy as well. It will be some time before this girl sees her money."

"She is heiress to another fortune which will be all her own when she reaches twenty-one. At the least, it amounts to more than a million."

"You expect me to believe that?" Jackson said incredulously.

"It's true. The wealth is from her dead mother, and the girl is the only living member of that family."

"But why should you want to betray your brother and his daughter?" Jackson asked. His tone was hard, but in truth he was becoming intrigued. As he listened, he was weighing the rewards — the several thousand dollars he could squeeze from this pitiful boy versus a million or more. It was hardly a choice.

"Brother and daughter — I owe them both a grudge," Arthur was saying. "You don't need the details. Just let us say that I can kill two birds with one stone, paying you off and getting my revenge at the same time. There is one condition, however. Follow my plan, and you must share the spoils when you succeed."

Jackson laughed, and the sound echoed in the deserted street. "So you want revenge, but you are not so desperate as to pass up an opportunity to profit. I knew there was a reason why I liked you, Arthur old man. Alright, tell me your plan."

"Not now. If I don't get back to my rooms, I'm bound to be caught and tossed out of school. Come to my apartment tomorrow morning at ten. My studious brother will be at his classes then, and there will be no chance of discovery."

"I shall be there, although I can see there is little reason I should trust you. Still, scoundrels must stick together. I will take my chances with you," Jackson replied.

They had reached a corner near the college. Arthur turned toward his apartment, and Jackson in the opposite direction.

"Sleep well, my boy," Jackson laughed as his steps retreated into the night.

Though Arthur managed to sneak back to his room with no difficulty, he did not sleep at all that night. His mind churned. Jackson had duped him, to be sure, but Arthur had no stomach for facing up to the fellow. He had promised a plan that would make them both rich, and now he had only a few hours in which to invent his scheme.

The next ten days passed very pleasantly in Lansdale. There were excursions to local points of interest, picnics in the hills with the King family, social visits with callers, musical evenings around Wealthy Stanhope's piano, and many quiet talks. Elsie became quite close to her aunt and to Lottie King and her older sister, Nettie. In fact, she was each day more reconciled to the prospect of remaining in Lansdale for the summer.

Horace's departure, however, was not easy, and Elsie almost regretted her decision. As she helped her father pack the last of his cases on the morning of his parting, she could not help but shed a few tears.

"Oh, Papa, I will miss you so much," she sighed.

"And I will miss you, dearest," Horace replied, putting a gentle arm around her shoulders. "But until I come back to reclaim you, let's do as we always have. We will write to each other every day. I want to hear all about what you and Aunt Wealthy are doing. You must tell me of your new friends, too, for I am sure you will meet more fine people in this lovely town. You know, Elsie, I'm very proud of you — that you are so grown and can take responsibility for yourself like this. If you need advice on anything, follow Aunt Wealthy's guidance and what you know to be my desires. I can trust you to behave just as you would if I were here with you."

"You can, Papa," Elsie said with confidence, "for I will always do my best to be faithful to your wishes."

"I know you will, my child," Horace said softly. Then he kissed her cheek and hugged her close.

As the morning train left the station with Horace aboard, Wealthy took her great-niece's hand and said, "Leave-taking is never easy, child, but I propose to lift your spirits with a little shopping. You haven't seen what our stores have to offer. Lansdale is not New York or Philadelphia, but I think you will find we are well stocked here for our needs."

"Thank you, Aunt Wealthy. I'd like to go shopping with you," Elsie replied.

The little woman — wearing an odd muslin dress and bonnet, carrying a large silk purse in one hand and a colorful parasol in the other — led her tall, beautiful, and fashionably attired niece into the shopping district of Lansdale. Their first stop was Over's Dry Goods.

"How are you today, Mr. Under?" Aunt Wealthy greeted the smiling merchant behind the counter.

"Over, if you please, Miss Stanhope. And I am quite well," he said, his eyes sparkling with amusement.

"Oh, you know my trouble with names," Wealthy said, although she was plainly untroubled by her mistake. "Have you any remnants of dress material today?"

"Some very nice pieces," the merchant said. He quickly gathered together a bundle of fabrics and spread the pieces on the counter. Wealthy chose six of the colorful remnants, plus a bolt of cotton shirting material, and Mr. Over promised to deliver them to her house that very morning.

This routine of selecting remnants was repeated in two more dry goods stores — between visits to the butcher and the bakery. Then they stopped at the dressmaker's shop where Wealthy purchased yet another half-dozen or so sturdy remnants from the woman's collection.

Leaving the neat little store, Elsie could contain her curiosity no longer. "Whatever will you do with all those remnants, Auntie?" she asked. "None of those pieces are large enough to make even a blouse for you or Phyllis, and you have no little people to dress."

"I don't, but other people do. I enjoy making children's clothes, and I will use the smallest bits for patchwork."

Suddenly understanding that her Aunt Wealthy's purchases would be used to benefit others, Elsie smiled and said, "Perhaps you will let us help you with your sewing. I'm competent with cutting and seaming, and Aunt Chloe's a marvel with needle and thread."

"Why, dear, I didn't invite you here to work, but if you would really like to help, it would be most appreciated," Aunt Wealthy said with a twinkle.

If Elsie thought she might be sad that day, she was not given the opportunity. Returning to Wealthy's house, they spied a woman on the front porch. She was dressed in bright colors and wore a slightly drooping feather in her straw hat. As they came up the walkway, the woman rushed forward, proclaiming in words that tumbled out, "I'm soooo sorry, Miss Stanhope, that I've been sooo long in calling upon your niece. It's not for want of courtesy. I've been away, nursing my sick sister in the country."

"It's good to see you, Mrs. Dime," Aunt Wealthy replied courteously.

"Excuse me, Nickle," the woman said.

"You are excused, though it's my mistake," Wealthy laughed. "And this is my great-niece, Miss Dinsmore. Elsie, this is Mrs. Di — Mrs. Nickle, who is our neighbor." Gesturing to the porch seats, Wealthy added, "Do be seated. I'm just sorry you arrived before we finished our shopping."

Mrs. Nickle's face flushed with embarrassment. "I'm terribly sorry," she stammered, "to call sooo early."

"Oh, no," Elsie hastened. "Auntie meant that she regrets we kept you waiting."

"Oh, dear, I do seem to have trouble getting my words turvy-topsy. Always putting the horse before the cart, as they say," Wealthy explained apologetically. "But tell us. Is your sister recovered?"

"She had rheumatism of the tonsils, but is better now. Lucky it wasn't the fever. They had a case of that where she lives, but he died."

Mrs. Nickle went on at some length with details of the funeral and her sister's tonsils. Just as she was explaining exactly how the tonsils were red and "infirmed," she suddenly asked, "Will you lend me your prescription for farmer's fruitcake, Miss Stanhope? It is the best thing you could ever eat, Miss Dinsmore."

"Of course, Mrs. — ah — Nickle. I will write out the recipe for you and send it over later today," Wealthy said.

Mrs. Nickle expressed her gratitude and after a little more conversation, she rose to leave, urging the ladies to call on her soon. As she was walking down the path, Lottie King entered the gate. The two passed with warm greetings, and Lottie bounded up the porch steps. She'd been invited to dinner, as part of Wealthy's campaign to keep Elsie's spirits high.

Wealthy excused herself to tend to something in the kitchen, and the girls adjourned to the sitting room.

"So you have met our peculiar currency," Lottie said in her lively manner.

"She is a Nickle and not a dime," Elsie laughed.

"A Nickle who never has a penny on her," Lottie replied. "I suppose she was borrowing something."

"A fruitcake recipe, though I doubt she must return it," Elsie said. "I found myself a little dizzy between Aunt Wealthy and Mrs. Nickle. I think I shall bring a dictionary the next time I meet with them. Can you tell me about our neighbor? Is there a better half in the Nickle house?"

"Shame on you, Elsie, for ever thinking a husband to be the *better* half. There was a Mr. Nickle to be sure, so I guess Aunt Wealthy's arithmetic is correct after all. Two Nickles would make a dime. But he died some years ago, and she alone is raising her children."

"That is no easy task," Elsie said with feeling.

"It's not," Lottie agreed, "and my mother often says that Mrs. Nickle is doing an admirable job. But we suspect that she hopes not to remain alone, for she has her eyes on a certain Mr. Wert — Mr. Was, as Aunt Wealthy calls him — who attends her church. And I mean literally that she had eyes on the poor man. Several Sundays back, Mrs. Nickle was walking home from church and Mr. Wert was in a group behind her. Well, she could not stop herself from looking backwards at him time and again until at last she walked straight into a lamp post! I'm afraid that everyone laughed, and she was dreadfully embarrassed."

"Poor woman," Elsie said seriously. "It's hardly following the Golden Rule to laugh at her discomfort."

"I know," Lottie agreed, "because apart from her borrowing and her strange use of words, she's a very good person and kind to everyone. But tell me, what else have you and Aunt Wealthy been up to today?"

There was such a contrast between the good-natured pastimes of Lansdale and the dark plot which had now been put in motion by Arthur Dinsmore and Tom Jackson.

On their first meeting after Arthur proposed his scheme, he had told Jackson more about the wealthy target of their fraud.

Hatching A Plot

"Her name is Elsie, and a prettier face you are unlikely to see anywhere, but her sweetness is too much for me to bear," Arthur said, not bothering to hide his distaste. "She has thwarted me with her obnoxious piety once too often."

"So I take it that an introduction from you would not serve me well," Jackson said.

"On the contrary, you must carefully conceal that you have any acquaintance with me. But an introduction is necessary. Luckily, my little brother maintains regular correspondence with our niece, so I am well aware of her situation. There could never be a better time to carry out this plan, for she is spending the summer with a dotty old aunt who lives alone in a small town in Ohio. Her father is there now, but will leave her in a few days. If he were around — well, he guards her with the ferocity of a lion, and even you would be no match for him."

"So we must strike while the iron is hot," Jackson sneered. "Now how do you propose to introduce me?"

"As it happens, Miss Stanhope, the crazy aunt, has an old friendship with a Mrs. Waters of this city. And Mrs. Waters's son Bob is a friend of mine."

Arthur opened his desk drawer and removed an envelope, "This is a letter of invitation which I received from Mrs. Waters some months ago. I don't know why I saved it, but here it is."

He handed the envelope to Jackson. "Inside you will find an excellent sample of that lady's handwriting. I believe you are adept at forging signatures. Can you do an entire letter?"

Jackson, who was examining the pages of the note, chuckled. "No problem, my man. No problem at all." Then his face clouded. "But what if the old aunt should write to this Mrs. Waters on the subject of my introduction. We would be found out."

"Luck is on our side, as I wish it had been on my side last night," Arthur replied. "Bob Waters told me that his mother is sailing for England next week and will be away until autumn. You should mention that in your letter, I think."

"Excellent," Jackson said, smiling broadly. "In Mrs. Waters's name then, I shall compose my introduction today. Come to my hotel this evening, and we will see if the wording meets your approval. It will take me a day or two to complete the 'copying' — I do hate that word 'forgery.' I have some business to complete here, but I should be able to begin my journey west in another week or so."

"No later than that," Arthur said urgently. "If her father should return for her before you secure her affections, you won't have a chance. He'll see through you in a second."

"And the girl?"

"Too innocent to spot a scoundrel at sight. But you must be very careful. If she suspects your true character, she will loathe you like a snake. She is religious beyond anyone I have ever known."

"Not very complimentary of you, my boy. But I dare say I can appear as moral and upright and respectful of religion as any man. Come to think of it, you may have something there. If she is so religious, then she may wish to convert me, to lead me from doubt as it were. Then she must love me as a fellow believer."

"Capital idea!" Arthur exclaimed. "You will appeal to her piety."

Hatching A Plot

And so, while Elsie and her Aunt Wealthy went about their days in Lansdale and Horace Dinsmore returned to his wife and son in Philadelphia, the cunning plot was hatched and set into motion.

CHAPTER

4

An Introduction for a Stranger

"They come to you in sheep's clothing, but inwardly they are ferocious wolves."

MATTHEW 7:15

"$\mathcal{I}$t's a magnificent gift, child," said Wealthy.

"Indeed it is, and so useful," added Lottie.

"I've never seen anything like it in my life," Phyllis declared.

"It sure is a beauty," Aunt Chloe agreed.

"It" was Elsie's present to her Aunt Wealthy — a sewing machine, the very best of its kind. It had just arrived from Cincinnati where it had been purchased, according to Elsie's specifications, by Horace. Now it sat in Wealthy's bedroom, with all the women gathered round it.

"I hope you like it," Elsie said, "I thought it would make your life a little easier in light of all the sewing you do."

Wealthy slipped her thin arm around Elsie's waist and hugged her niece. "Oh, it will, dear child. I could not have asked for a better present. We must try it right now."

Lottie immediately volunteered to be the first to make the experiment, and after a few false starts — the girl tended to rock the treadle with a bit too much of her natural exuberance — she was soon making neat rows of stitches on a scrap piece of muslin.

"Have you ever seen the like? Look how fast that needle goes," Phyllis said in amazement. "Why, Miss Wealthy, you'll be able to run up those little children's dresses in no time with this."

"And the shirts you make for Harry Duncan, too," said Lottie.

"He has just written that his last set of shirts are going wonderfully fast, so I must be cutting him up more,"

Wealthy said in her usual confusion. "Oh, Elsie, this is so exciting. And look at us, just like kittens with a new ball of yarn!"

Elsie was delighted with the reaction to her gift. She had learned to operate her Mamma's sewing machine at The Oaks and knew how one could lighten her great-aunt's burden. She had pondered some time about giving a practical present rather than something more lavish, but she'd decided, after getting to know Wealthy, that practical was what the little woman appreciated. And Horace had agreed, stopping in Cincinnati to order the machine on his way to Philadelphia.

"I am sure we are the only family in Lansdale with such a treasure," Wealthy said.

"Probably in all Ohio," Lottie declared. "Well, maybe not *all* Ohio, but they must be very rare. Come try it, Aunt Wealthy. It's easier than it looks, once you get the peddle right. Elsie can show you how to guide the cloth without nipping your fingers."

Phyllis and Chloe excused themselves to tend to their chores, and Wealthy and the two girls continued to work at the machine, Elsie explaining how to thread the bobbin and the best way to run the cloth under the needle to get straight stitches.

"What you got there?" came a voice at the doorway that led onto Wealthy's private patio.

"Willy!" exclaimed Wealthy with a start, for she was not expecting the interruption. "It's a sewing machine. Now, what can I do for you, child?"

"Mamma asks if she could have a little lightning to raise her bread," the little girl answered, peering around Wealthy to see the strange contraption.

"Yeast? Why, you go on to see Phyllis, and ask her for yeast. She'll give you what your mother needs."

Willy, still fascinated by the machine that Lottie was now pumping like a church organ, hesitated. "Oh, there's a man at your front door," she said, and at just that instant the doorbell rang. The women all turned to stare at Willy.

"Are you a mind reader, child?" Wealthy asked.

Willy smiled — a bright grin that crinkled her freckled nose and revealed two missing teeth. "No, ma'am. I just saw him coming in the front gate behind me. That's all. But he looks like a gentleman."

Chloe entered and presented a letter to Wealthy. The lady adjusted her spectacles and broke the wax seal on the envelope. Quickly, she perused the missive, giving commentary as she read. "It's a letter of introduction from my good friend Alma Waters. Let's see, she wishes me to treat the young man with all the courtesy and kindness I would show her own son for she holds him in high esteem, and etcetera and so forth." Looking up at Chloe she asked, "What have you done with him?"

"Set him down in the parlor, Miss Wealthy."

"Good. Will you take Willy into the kitchen, Chloe, and see that she gets some yeast for her mother. I'll tend to this young man."

As Chloe led the curious Willy Nickle away, Wealthy removed her glasses, patted her gray hair, and consulted the letter once again. "Alma says that his name is Bromly Edgerton. Quite romantic sounding, don't you girls think?"

Lottie cast a gleeful look at Elsie, as Wealthy left the room.

In the parlor, Wealthy found a handsome and well-dressed young man who came forward to greet her with mannerly ease and grace.

"Miss Stanhope, I presume," he said.

"I am, sir. And you are Mr. Siderton. Please be seated."

"Thank you, madam, but let me help you to a seat first. Please pardon the correction, but Edgerton is my name."

"Of course it is," Wealthy said as she took her place on the couch and Mr. Edgerton reclaimed his chair. "For the sake of my good friend Mrs. Waters, I welcome you to Lansdale. Tell me, sir, do you expect to stay long in our town?"

"Well, madam, I had no such expectation before I arrived, but I find Lansdale to be such a pretty place that I think I may do no better. You see, Miss Stanhope, I have been somewhat exhausted by my business this last year, and my physician ordered me to get out of the city, find good country air, and relax for a time. I do believe that your charming town meets all his requirements."

"Lansdale is certainly clean and relaxing." Wealthy responded. "Small by city standards, but not lacking in attractions."

"I look forward to the attractions of Lansdale, but I must get settled first. Can you recommend a boarding place? Some quiet, private hotel, perhaps, where drinking and that kind of thing do not go on. I am unused to such behavior and find it revolting."

"I'm glad to hear you say so, young man. Such sentiments do you honor. And I believe I can recommend a place that will suit you. I daresay Mrs. Dime — that is Mrs. Nickle, who lives just opposite here — would be glad to provide for you. She mentioned recently that she would like to have one or two gentlemen boarders."

"Ah," Edgerton said, a soft smile playing on his handsome face. "The location would suit me well. And you think she could give me comfortable accommodations?"

"Oh, yes. She has very pleasant rooms and is an excellent cook."

"A widow?"

"Yes, and in her middle years. She has two children, but they are of an age not to annoy you. Mrs. Nickle is most suitable for a landlady — neat, industrious, honest, obliging, though perhaps not an intellectual companion."

Edgerton laughed, "If she is all you say, then I can forgo intellectual company." He leaned forward slightly and with a charming smile, added, "unless you could find it in your kind heart to take me into this lovely home of yours."

Wealthy smiled back but shook her head decidedly. "No, sir, I have a guest and need no other. Besides, I believe that men require a good deal more care and attention than I am ready to give at my age."

Edgerton sat back and said in an apologetic manner, "Excuse me, my dear madam, for taking such an unwarranted liberty by asking. I beg ten thousand pardons."

"That is a great many," Wealthy replied sweetly, "but consider them all granted. Tell me, is my friend Mrs. Waters well? I must finish reading her letter and reply to her immediately."

"She is quite well and on her way to England. Perhaps she mentions her trip in the letter, for she sailed on the day after she wrote it. I understood that she will be away for several months."

Elsie's Stolen Heart

Wealthy nodded politely and answered several more of the young man's somewhat long-winded questions about the town and the region. But she was beginning to wish he would leave. Edgerton, however, lingered in hopes of catching sight of Elsie. But when the girl did not appear, he finally rose to depart. At the door, he asked to be directed to Mrs. Nickle's, and Wealthy noticed that he proceeded directly there.

When she returned to her room, Lottie greeted her with a laugh. "Really, Aunt Wealthy," the girl said, "we were starting to suspect that you had eloped with your gentleman caller."

"Don't be silly," Wealthy said with a touch of irritation, "though I believe he might have stayed to dinner if good manners did not prevent him."

"Who is he?" Lottie asked. "Is he young and handsome?"

"You are too inquisitive for your own good, Lottie King," Wealthy said with a little laugh and a twinkle in her eye. "But, yes, he is young and handsome. Tall and dark too. And a talker, I'd say. But a gentleman to all appearances. In his middle twenties."

"Do you advise me to set my cap for him?" Lottie teased.

"No, I do not. Though he may improve on further acquaintance."

"Well, anyway," Lottie went on, "I don't approve of marrying. Do you, Aunt Wealthy? You've never married, and I'm sure you have had lots of chances."

"It is not a question of approving," the old lady said quietly. "I had offers, it's true, and one of them I accepted." An uncharacteristic look of sadness came into her eyes as she continued, "I would have happily married him, but others intervened, and the match was broken off. No, dears, don't follow my example. When the right man comes along, marry him."

"But surely not if our parents refuse their consent," Elsie spoke up in some surprise.

"Oh, no," Wealthy said. "It is those who follow the Fifth Commandment to whom God promises long life and prosperity."

"And those who love their parents find it so easy to obey them," Elsie said softly, thinking of her Papa.

"On the contrary, child," Wealthy replied wistfully. "Loving our parents can sometimes make it very hard."

Elsie wanted to ask what her great-aunt meant, for the girl found this last statement confusing, but Lottie piped up, "You must have lots of suitors, Elsie — a girl as beautiful and smart and wealthy as you."

Elsie blushed and said nothing.

"Come on. Am I not right?" Lottie persisted. "Haven't you had offers?"

"Several," Elsie admitted, "but Papa says that money has strong attractions for most men."

"May the Lord protect you from all men who marry for money!" Wealthy exclaimed suddenly. "I sometimes think that wealth is an affliction and a curse."

"I know that it is a great responsibility," Elsie said with a look of gravity. But after a moment's pause, her face lighted once more. "Will you and Lottie excuse me for a little while?" she asked, rising from her chair and laying the collar she was sewing aside. "I want to finish my letter to Papa, then I'll return for more stitching and chatting."

Bromly Edgerton — the alias chosen by Tom Jackson for just the romantic quality that Wealthy Stanhope had noticed — found that Mrs. Nickle and her home met his exact purposes.

The woman was indeed anxious to have a boarder, and Edgerton could tell that the extra income would be useful to her. When he informed her that he had come at Miss Stanhope's suggestion, Mrs. Nickle immediately accepted him as the right sort and gave him the choice of two fine rooms. Both rooms were sizable, with comfortable furnishings and cheerful decor. But the room at the front of the house, with its window that looked upon the Stanhope place, was his obvious choice.

Mrs. Nickle was showing the features of the room when she directed him to come to that very window.

"The view is beautiful," she said slyly. "Don't you agree?"

He looked out, and his eyes were immediately attracted to a second-story window in the house opposite. A young woman, as beautiful as the dawn, stood in the window, framed as if in a portrait.

"Who is she?" Edgerton asked.

"Miss Stanhope's great-niece, here for a visit," Mrs. Nickle replied. She intended no harm but was always happy to be the first with a bit of gossip. "She's from the South and worth a mint of money, as they say. Isn't she handsome?"

"Handsome doesn't express it," Edgerton said a little breathlessly. "She is angelic! Ah, but she's gone now."

"Well, you'll see her again soon enough, and all the young ladies that flitter in and out of Miss Stanhope's — like Miss Lottie and Miss Nettie."

"And they are?"

"The Kings. Daughters of Dr. King and his wife who live next door to Miss Stanhope. They're distant cousins of the old lady, I believe. And pretty girls they are, too, all spry and full of energivity like young colts. They're getting thick as thieves with Miss Elsie, but they don't hold a candle to her, least as far as beauty goes. Well, what do you say to the room?"

Turning from the window, Edgerton replied with enthusiasm, "I'll take it right now and pay you three weeks' rent to start. Can you arrange to have my luggage brought from the station?"

"I'll have your bags here in an hour," Mrs. Nickle promised. "You just make yourself comfortable now. Dinner'll be on the table at one o'clock. And, Mr. Edgerton," she added as she went to the door, "welcome to Lansdale."

A fine welcome it was, Bromly Edgerton thought to himself as he lay back on the bed of his rented room and gazed toward the front window. So far, all had gone according to plan. Better than he'd expected, in fact, for he would not have guessed he'd find himself located so close to his prey.

"I did rather well with the old lady," he thought. "She seems easy enough to win over with a smile and a bit of flattering."

But the girl? Arthur has said she was a beauty, but Edgerton had not expected such an exquisite creature. Face, figure — yes, he was going to enjoy winning her affections. But he had to approach this carefully. He'd made a good start with the aunt today; it was important to get her on his side first. And what about these King girls? Small town girls, but they were a doctor's daughters, educated, and probably not so naive as one might expect. They could be a problem if they sensed anything amiss. Yes, he must court them as well, to the point where they trusted him and would vouch for him to their new friend. When he had won everyone's trust, then he could go after the prize. It would take a bit of doing, but Edgerton had every confidence in his charms.

He laughed to himself. Mrs. Nickle. She would be a fine ally and never even know it. His landlady seemed to have a horde of information that he could turn to his advantage, and she liked to talk.

The real difficulty was time. Edgerton knew that the father might return at any moment and that no amount of charm would win him over. Arthur had warned repeatedly that Horace Dinsmore was a man of the world who could spot a fraud after two minutes' conversation. Not a few young men had attempted to pay their suit to the girl and her fortune, only to be driven off by the father.

"I must win her heart before he knows I'm alive," Edgerton thought. That meant insinuating himself into the Stanhope household as quickly as possible. He must seek the first opportunity to call again.

His chance came sooner than expected. After dinner (and Mrs. Nickle proved to be as good a cook as advertised), Edgerton was in his room unpacking his cases, when there was a knock at his door, and a freckled-face girl entered.

"I'm Lenwilla Ellawea Nickle," she said bluntly. "Simon — that's Miss Stanhope's servant boy — brought this over for you."

She stuck out her hand, bearing a small envelope, and when Edgerton took it, she turned and marched out of the room without another word.

After closing the door, Edgerton eagerly opened the envelope, read the enclosed note, and smiled. It was an invitation. Some neighbors would be stopping in at Miss Stanhope's home that evening, and the lady expressed her wish that Mr. Edgerton might join them at eight o'clock.

"How perfect," Edgerton chuckled to himself. "That odd, old lady is doing my work for me."

CHAPTER

5

Setting
The Trap

*"With his mouth each speaks
cordially to his neighbor,
but in his heart he sets
a trap for him."*

JEREMIAH 9:8

Setting The Trap

*E*dgerton's first evening at Miss Stanhope's could not have gone better. His hostess introduced him, in her inimitable way, to several of Lansdale's most influential citizens. The town's mayor was there — a Mr. Barnwell whom Wealthy introduced as "Mr. Farmgood" — and the good man welcomed Edgerton with a hearty handshake. Mr. and Mrs. Goings, who owned the town's hotel, were presented as "Mr. and Mrs. Comings." An elderly widow named Mrs. Winters became "Mrs. Summers," though she was too deaf to hear Wealthy's mistake. The Kings were, as usual, introduced as "Princes."

Wealthy apologized for her "problems with names," but Edgerton assured her that it was simply a charming habit that demonstrated an inventive turn of mind. In truth, he cared nothing for these people or their names. Only one face did he look for in the crowd. When he met Elsie, however, he was for the briefest moment struck speechless. Close before his eyes, she was even lovelier than the vision he had seen from his window; her voice was like the liquid essence of the South, and her hospitable greetings to him were as gracious as they were genuine.

He noticed that several young men of the town were paying their court to the beautiful heiress, yet their ardor gave him no concern. He could outshine those country bumpkins, he thought with supreme confidence. But tonight, he was determined to ingratiate himself with Wealthy Stanhope, and by calculated attentiveness, he achieved his objective. His manners were perfection, assuring Wealthy that he was, indeed, a gentleman. And his conversation was fascinating, for Edgerton had in fact traveled widely and seen much of the world. His stories of experiences in Europe and South America proved delightful to a woman who read much but traveled very little. Edgerton was also careful not to be too forward and to listen more than he spoke, so that Wealthy quickly revised her first impression that he was an excessively talkative young man. By the time he was ready to depart (and he made sure to be among the early leave-takers), Wealthy was completely under his spell.

"You must feel free to call on us when you are at leisure," she told him as he was thanking her for the pleasant evening. "You are very near my niece's age, I think, and would make good company for her and the young Kings. They cannot possibly enjoy spending all their time with an old lady."

Edgerton reacted to this statement with feigned surprise. "Why, Miss Stanhope, you are one of the most interesting and entertaining ladies I have ever met," he said. "But if your niece and the young ladies are interested, I should certainly appreciate joining them on occasion."

The first such occasion came the very next morning when Edgerton happened, by design, to be exiting Mrs. Nickle's gate as the King girls were walking toward Mrs. Stanhope's.

"Mr. Edgerton!" called out Lottie, who never stood on ceremony. "Where are you headed this glorious summer day?"

"Ah, Miss Lottie and Miss Nettie. Good day to you," he replied with a slight bow and then casually crossed the street to share a few words. "I'm going to the stables to arrange for a horse to ride during my stay."

"You are a skilled horseman, I imagine," said Nettie.

"How skilled I am is a question for the horse," Edgerton replied lightly, "but I do love to ride, and your fields and hills seem to offer excellent grounds for exercise."

"For riding and walking," Nettie agreed. "Nature has blessed us with a variety of interesting sights."

"I say," Lottie interjected, "we were about to ask Elsie to take a walk this afternoon. Would you care to join us?"

"I would indeed, if it meets everyone's approval," Edgerton replied.

"That's no problem," Lottie laughed, and in a lowered voice, she added, "You seem to have wrapped Aunt Wealthy around your finger last night."

"Lottie! Don't be so rude," Nettie exclaimed.

But Edgerton only laughed. "Your sister has it wrong, Miss King, for it was Miss Stanhope who enchanted me. Such a charming woman she is, and so unusual in her independence."

"What do you think of her manner of dress?" asked Lottie, who could never quite contain her curiosity.

Edgerton thought for a moment. "It's a little old-fashioned by the standards of ordinary taste," he responded, "but in Paris there are great ladies who choose to be individual in their dress and thereby set the fashions. In fact, I think Miss Stanhope may be ahead, rather than behind the times."

"Bravo, Mr. Edgerton," said Lottie, clapping her hands. "You have seen what we already know — that Aunt Wealthy is an exceptional woman."

"But we asked Mr. Edgerton to join us for our walk this afternoon," Nettie said, bringing the conversation back to

practical matters. Addressing the tall, young man, she suggested, "Perhaps you will meet us here after dinner today."

"I will, and I thank you very much for the invitation," he replied, smiling charmingly. "Now, I must leave you and continue my quest for a horse."

"'My kingdom for a horse,'" Lottie laughed as Edgerton walked away and the two girls entered the gate.

"I remember those words, Lottie. What are they from?" Nettie inquired when Edgerton was out of earshot.

"Shakespeare, dear Sister. They are the words of Richard the Third."

"But wasn't he an evil king?"

"Mr. Shakespeare thought so," Lottie said, "but I spoke the quote only as words about the value of a horse, not as a reflection upon Mr. Edgerton. Our new visitor to Lansdale reminds me more of a handsome knight."

The walk that afternoon began many days in which Edgerton accompanied Lottie, Nettie, and Elsie in their activities. When the weather was favorable, the four would ride together in the open countryside or walk the nearby woods. Several times they enjoyed picnics — packed by the girls with Phyllis and Chloe's help. On inclement days, they would gather on Wealthy's broad front porch to play chess and card games while the summer rain fell. On one wet afternoon, Elsie, having received a book that day from her father, suggested that they read aloud. Edgerton volunteered to take the first turn, and all three girls as well as Aunt Wealthy were mesmerized by his mellifluous voice.

Wealthy was frankly delighted by the attention Edgerton paid to her niece and the other girls. She had worried that her own life style was too much of a set pattern to keep a young woman entertained for an entire summer, and she had initially counted on Lottie and Nettie to supply diversions. The addition of Mr. Edgerton to their group, she was relieved to discover, seemed an entirely wholesome one. To her eye, Edgerton was a more than acceptable companion for the young ladies and a welcome guardian on their excursions.

Edgerton had cemented his favor with Wealthy on his first Sunday in Lansdale, seeking out the church that she and the Kings attended. He made a point to associate only with townspeople whom he knew to be approved by the elderly lady. Through these associations, Edgerton soon learned that Wealthy, for all her strangeness, was highly esteemed by her friends and neighbors and regarded by one and all as a leading member of the community. From Mrs. Nickle, he learned that Wealthy was, true to her name, quite well-off. "Miss Stanhope inherited a pile from her old pappy," Mrs. Nickle confided, "but she's not anywhere like so rich as that pretty niece of hers. I hear that Miss Elsie will come into millions when she's of age, and she's also got properties and a plantation down in New Orleans."

Edgerton contrived to be with Elsie and her friends as often as possible, and he was careful to pay equal attention to all the girls at the outset. But he didn't make himself too freely available. There were several evenings when he politely declined Wealthy's supper invitations. Edgerton understood too well that no man ever suffered from a hint of mystery and that his absences would intrigue Elsie. She was not, he judged, a silly young woman or likely to fall for an overly ardent suitor.

And what was Elsie's opinion of him? In the beginning, she found the dark stranger not to her liking, though she could not explain her reaction even to herself. It was an instinctive feeling — an emotion that troubled her because it seemed unfair and uncharitable. Gradually, however, she grew to enjoy Edgerton's company. His obvious learning and impeccable manners, his ability to converse on a wide range of subjects that interested her, his affable personality, and most of all, his apparent Christian commitment appealed to her good nature. She forgot her first impressions and was sincerely glad when in his presence. And she found herself missing his company when he was not around. Sensing the change in her attitude, Edgerton began to tighten his web. In the subtlest of ways, he would single Elsie out, showing her little preferences and special attentions.

His only source of anxiety came from a custom that he observed each morning from his bedroom window. At ten o'clock, Simon would leave the Stanhope house, returning about a half hour later with the day's mail. Elsie would always be waiting on the porch, and at Simon's approach, she would rush to him, receive an envelope, then, with her face aglow, return to the house. And each day, usually within an hour, she would leave the house for her morning walk into the town, and always she carried another envelope.

Edgerton, having observed this ritual a number of times, came to the conclusion that such regular correspondence indicated the existence of a rival suitor, for he could think of no other reason for a young woman to be so dedicated to the daily mail. The possibility worried him considerably, and he even thought about stealing one of the letters in order to confirm his suspicions.

In the end, however, he managed to be at the Stanhope gate one morning when Simon arrived with the envelope. As Elsie took it from the boy's hand, Edgerton jested, "It is a fortunate man whose letter can bring such a look of delight to your face, Miss Dinsmore. A man who is after your heart, perhaps?"

Elsie smiled. "A man who already has my heart," she replied with good humor. But seeing the shadow that fell over Edgerton's face at her remark, she explained, "It's from my father. We correspond every day."

Edgerton was greatly relieved, but this information also raised a new concern. Had she written to her father about himself?

"I see," Edgerton said with a little laugh. "But what can you possibly find to write to your father each and every day?"

"There is plenty to tell about. Papa wants to know how I am spending my time, where I've gone, what new friends I've made, what books I'm reading, and how I like them."

"The books or the friends?" Edgerton asked in a studiously careless manner.

"Both. I tell him everything. My Papa is my confidant and my best friend in the world."

"So you go to the post office every day?"

"Every day but the Sabbath when we are commanded to rest and refrain from worldly activities."

"You must be very strict keepers of the Sabbath."

"No more strict than the Bible teaches us we should be."

Edgerton paused for a moment, then said, "I would think such observance would be tiresome and tedious for you. Don't you become bored?"

"Oh, no," Elsie replied gravely, "for the Sabbath is to me the happiest day of the week."

Edgerton wanted a bit more information, so he remarked jokingly, "Perhaps it is Miss Stanhope who keeps you so strictly to the rules while your father is far away."

Elsie lowered her eyes and said softly, "Not at all, sir. I would obey my Papa and my Heavenly Father even if I were alone in a deserted place. I never want to be a hypocrite in my faith. And because I love my father and my God, it's never a hardship to follow their commands."

Realizing that his jesting had been taken in earnest by the girl, Edgerton quickly said, "I beg your pardon, Miss Dinsmore. I meant nothing by my little joke, for I greatly respect your devotion to your parent and your beliefs."

Elsie looked up into his face, and reading his expression as genuinely apologetic, she smiled sweetly and said, "There is no need for you to ask my pardon, sir. I understand your questions, for there are many dedicated Christians who do not practice their faith in the same way as I and my family."

"And daughters who do not obey their fathers from such honest affection," Edgerton added in a serious tone. "Believe me, Miss Dinsmore, you have my deepest admiration."

Then he took his leave, for he could see she was anxious to get to her letter. But the incident, while it explained the correspondence, had left him a little shaken. He had feared another suitor, but he now wondered if his rival might not be more dangerous. If the girl did tell her father everything, she had surely mentioned Edgerton in her letters. What had she said? Had she mentioned anything that might give him away to her scrupulous Papa? In his black heart, Edgerton resolved to speed up his courtship and to claim the girl before that father smelled a rat.

CHAPTER

6

New Experiences

"The Lord does not look at the things man looks at. Man looks at the outward appearance, but the Lord looks at the heart."

1 Samuel 16:7

$\mathcal{E}$lsie, Lottie, and Wealthy were in the kitchen helping Phyllis with her dinner preparations when a familiar voice was heard at the door.

"My Mamma wants to know can she borrow a cup of vinegar," said Willy Nickle, holding a china teacup before her face. "And she says can the young ladies come over to our house tonight after supper for a little party."

"Is the vinegar for the party?" Lottie asked. "It will make a strange punch if it is."

Willy shot a doubtful look at the girl. "You're joking with me, aren't you, Miss Lottie? The vinegar's for the gentleman boarder's salad. Mamma's baking good stuff for the party."

"Who will be there, dear?" Wealthy asked as she took the teacup from Willy and went into the pantry for the vinegar crock.

"Not too many folks," the little girl said, following Wealthy. "Some young ladies and gentlemen that Mamma thought Miss Elsie would like to meet."

Shyly, she tugged at Wealthy's sleeve and whispered, "Mamma particularly wants Miss Elsie and Miss King and her sister to come. Do you think they will?"

Smiling, Wealthy said, "I will do my best to coax them, and you can tell your mother they will attend. Here now, take your vinegar. And walk carefully, or you will spill it."

When the little girl had gone, Wealthy said, "Well, it seems you girls have an engagement this evening."

"But Aunt Wealthy," Elsie said in surprise, "you can't expect me to go there?"

"Why not, dear?"

"Mrs. Nickle is not the kind of lady Papa would want me to closely associate with. He's very particular about such matters."

Wealthy turned to her niece, and there was a undertone of sternness in her voice as she spoke. "I appreciate your father's concerns, my dear, but while Mrs. Nickle is not refined, she is a clever, hard-working, and honest Christian woman. I know she looks forward to your attendance and will be very hurt if you stay away. She has always been a good and considerate neighbor to me, and I would be grateful if you go this evening. You do not need to stay late."

"And it will be a good time," Lottie assured, taking Elsie's hand. "Everyone likes Mrs. Nickle and her funny ways. You will meet only nice people there."

Elsie was still not certain, but Wealthy said kindly, "Remember, Elsie, that very few people have had your advantages. Mrs. Nickle has made the very best of her lot in life, and while she may lack your manners and education, she is no less a lady deserving respect. Trust me, child, your father would approve of your accepting her invitation."

Remembering Horace's instructions that she should follow her aunt's guidance, Elsie said, "Then I will go, to please you, Auntie."

"I'm glad that's settled," Lottie said gaily. "And you must come to our house before the party. Nettie has talked me into trying a new hairdo, and I'd like your opinion of it before I make a public appearance."

"I'll be glad to give you my thoughts, but I'm not so sure I can be the best judge," Elsie said.

"Oh, pooh," Lottie snorted. "You have wonderful taste in fashions, Elsie, and I trust your judgment. But look at the clock. Mother will be waiting dinner for me if I don't hurry. Come over tonight after supper."

"I will," Elsie called out as her friend dashed away.

After their dinner, Elsie and her aunt went to the little, stone patio off Wealthy's bedroom. The patio was deeply shaded and provided a cool retreat from the afternoon sun. Wealthy had her sewing basket for she wanted to darn some stockings, and Elsie carried a sketch book in which she had been collecting drawings of interesting wildflowers during her walks. She was using colored pencils to re-do one of her rough sketches.

They worked and chatted in the agreeable way of people who had become completely at ease in one another's company.

"I've been thinking about Mrs. Nickle," Elsie said, "and you are right, Auntie. It's very kind of her to have this party, but I wonder why she cares to since she must do all the hard work by herself."

"But Elsie, dear, not many have servants to tend to their wants as you and I do. In a small town such as this and on the farms, there are many good families like the Nickles who work hard from dawn to dusk for what must seem to you to be small material rewards. But they are quite happy with their share of God's blessings.

"Do you remember what Paul said to the Thessalonians? 'Make it your ambition to lead a quiet life, to mind your own business and to work with your hands,'" she quoted, "'so that your daily life will win the respect of outsiders and so that you will not be dependent on anybody.' I believe that's what Mrs. Nickle is striving to do, though she may have a little difficulty with minding her own business at times. But she works very hard, my dear, and while her household may seem very strange to you, she leads an altogether decent and respectable life."

"I can see that," Elsie agreed. "I'm afraid that for all the traveling Papa and I have done, I live a very sheltered life."

"Perhaps, my dear, but you have an open heart and a good mind. You will learn," Wealthy said reassuringly. "But I must warn you that I believe you are to be the center of attention tonight."

"I am?"

"Well, dear, none of us are immune to a little pride now and then. I think that Mrs. Nickle will gain some honor in our little community for being hostess to the rich heiress from the South," Wealthy chuckled softly.

Elsie look amused, but her expression turned serious as she replied, "It's rather humbling to be valued principally for one's wealth."

"Yes, I understand," her aunt said. "I've experienced the same feeling. But those who really know you do not measure you by your fortune. Though Dr. King is not a rich man by any means, he and his family look upon you as no more or less than a dear, sweet, new friend. Your presence has brought much joy to Lottie and Nettie, and they would do anything for you. As for myself — dear girl, I can hardly bear to think that you must leave me, though I know your father will be grateful for your return."

New Experiences

"I wish we could take you with us, Auntie. You would so enjoy my Mamma Rose and little Trip," Elsie said as she placed her soft hand over her aunt's. "I've often envied my friend Lucy Carrington for her loving grandparents. I never had a grandmother, you know, because Papa's stepmother never accepted me as her own. But you have taken that place now, Aunt Wealthy."

"I wish my own sister had lived to see and know you, child," Wealthy sighed, and two, small tears trembled at the corners of her eyes. "She was a wonderful woman and would have loved you with her whole heart. But I shall be proud to serve in her stead."

Elsie rose and went to embrace her aunt. She hugged the tiny, fragile woman lightly, kissed her wrinkled cheek, and said in a voice low with emotion, "Thank you, Auntie."

Wealthy returned the hug warmly; then she bent to her sewing basket and fumbled for a handkerchief. Dabbing quickly at her eyes, she said briskly, "I think I'm ready for my afternoon siesta. At my age, it is a necessity. But you might want a little nap yourself, Elsie. Remember, I promised Horace that I would keep you in perfect health."

Elsie laughed. "Poor Papa has never quite forgotten a time when I was ill. But I'm really not tired. I think I'll go to my room and write to him. Then I can finish this drawing. It is intended as a gift for a friend."

Elsie's Stolen Heart

When Elsie appeared at the Kings' door that evening, she was welcomed in by Mrs. King. "I'm glad you're here. The girls are in Nettie's room," the good woman said with a laugh and a shake of her head, "and the heavens only know what they are doing with their hair. I do believe Lottie would wear a bird cage on her head if she thought it would make an adventure. Go on in, Elsie, and try to keep them within the bounds of propriety."

Smiling at Mrs. King's imagery, Elsie was pleased to discover on entering Nettie's pretty bedroom, that neither of her friends was wearing a bird cage. Nettie, in fact, looked quite charming with her hair swept up and her soft curls held in combs. But she was struggling with her sister's heavy, dark locks.

"It's really unfair," Lottie complained, "that you two are blessed with those natural curls and I have this uncooperative head of sheep's wool."

"Your hair is lovely," Elsie protested. "It doesn't curl, that's true, but it is so thick, and it waves beautifully."

"The problem," Nettie said as she bent over her sister's head and tried to secure several straggling strands with a comb, "is that her hair is like the rest of her. It simply does not want to behave in the expected fashion."

Elsie took a seat on the bed to watch this Herculean struggle.

"You're lucky, my friend," Lottie said. "You have your wonderful Chloe to do your toilette."

"Why, I was just thinking how much I admire your independence," Elsie replied, "and feeling ashamed of my own helplessness."

"Have you never done your own hair?" Nettie asked in surprise.

"Never."

"Or dressed yourself?"

"Not without Aunt Chloe's assistance. I've never put on even stockings or shoes without her help," Elsie said, her face flushing. She had never considered her own helplessness before, and the thought truly mortified her.

"Well, it's rather nice to be able to do things for yourself," Lottie said complacently. A lock of her dark hair chose that moment to fall from its place and dangle in front of her eye. She blew at it angrily and declared. "But I could use Chloe's assistance at this moment."

"I have an idea," Elsie said. "Leave your hair, Lottie, and finish getting dressed. Then come over to our house and let Aunt Chloe finish your hair. She'll be happy to do it. Then we can all go to the party together. What do you say?"

"That's perfect!" Lottie exclaimed. "I was beginning to believe my only hope was a wig."

Nettie sat on the bed next to Elsie as Lottie rushed to her own room to put on her party dress.

"What is it like to have someone like Chloe?" Nettie asked. "I don't mean to pry, but I admit to the family trait of curiosity. We have servants here, but not slaves. I was wondering what it is like?"

"I'm not sure what to tell you," Elsie answered slowly. "I've never understood why some people are slaves, but I've never known any other way. Aunt Chloe has been with me since I was born. She has always loved me and cared for me and protected me."

"Like a mother?"

"Almost, though you know my mother died just days after my birth. Aunt Chloe kept my mother's image and memory alive for me from the beginning, so I never thought of her as my mother. But you are right, Nettie. Aunt Chloe could not love me more if I were her own daughter."

"Has she no family of her own?"

"None that I know of," Elsie said and was inwardly shocked that this question had never occurred to her before.

Nettie became aware of the change in Elsie's expression; the visitor's face was serious and her brow wrinkled in deep thought.

"Well, you are lucky to have such a loving companion," Nettie said cheerfully, and she rose from the bed, pulling Elsie up with her. "Come now. Let's find out what is taking Lottie so long. Perhaps she's become entangled in her dress, and we will have to straighten her out."

Elsie laughed, and her face regained its cheerful look.

Not many minutes later, all three girls were in the Stanhope kitchen. Lottie was seated in a straight, wooden chair, and a soft towel was draped about her shoulders. Chloe, her mouth full of hairpins and a brush in her hand, was busily sweeping the girl's rich mane into a regal hair style that was both fashionable and complimentary to her young face.

"You are a wonder," Nettie declared in admiration of Chloe's skills.

The nursemaid was putting the finishing touches to her handiwork when they heard the doorbell ring. Chloe instantly started to lay her tools down, but Elsie put a gently restraining hand on her arm. "You're busy

here, Aunt Chloe," the girl said. "Aunt Wealthy is in the garden and Phyllis is feeding the chickens. There's no need to disturb any of you when I am capable of answering the door."

She hurried from the room, feeling a little elated at this small act of independence. Reaching the front door, she beheld a familiar figure.

"Mr. Edgerton."

"Miss Dinsmore. I came over to ask if I might escort you to the party," Edgerton said, his face handsome in the glow of the lamplight.

"Thank you, sir. In fact, there are three to escort, for Lottie and Nettie are here, too. Will you come into the parlor and wait?" Elsie asked as she gestured him inside. "We need just a few minutes to be ready. What time does Mrs. Nickle expect us?"

"As soon as you arrive," Edgerton laughed, "for you are her special guest, and your aunt has informed her that you must take your leave at ten o'clock. Mrs. Nickle, I believe, covets every minute of your attention. I must say, I understand her feeling."

"That is kind of her," Elsie said nonchalantly, ignoring his last remark.

"Do you always keep such early hours?" he asked as she led him to the parlor.

"As a rule, yes. My father believes it is necessary for good health."

"And beauty," he added with a charming little bow.

"I hope we are not unfashionably early," Lottie giggled as their little group approached Mrs. Nickle's porch.

"I hear a number of voices, so we are not the first," Edgerton said.

"I've never understood that idea of being 'fashionably late,'" Nettie commented. "It seems mere rudeness to me."

The door opened, and Mrs. Nickle — in bright attire with ribbons streaming and eyes glowing — beamed at them in delight.

"Come in! Come in!" she called. "I'm powerfully glad you are here so early. My, you girls are a sight to behold. Such charming dresses and hair! Now come into my parlor, and I will introduce you."

There were five or six young men and women in the neat room, and the introductions were quickly accomplished. While the guests chatted, a girl and a boy — both decked out in their Sunday best — observed from their perches on a window seat.

Elsie, politely excusing herself from the adult conversation, moved to the children.

"Hello, Willy," she said warmly. "How lovely you look tonight. Is this your brother?"

"Yes ma'am, this is Binny."

Elsie bent forward a little and looked into the boy's small, serious face.

"How are you, Binny?" she asked sweetly.

"Fine," he said, though his lips barely moved to speak and his expression remained as stony as granite.

"He doesn't talk much," Willy explained. "He's like our Pappy in that way."

"Well, Binny, perhaps you might talk with me a little later," Elsie said, keeping her eyes and her smile on the solemn child. He stared at her for several seconds, and then that faintest hint of movement crept onto his lips. "Fine," he said at last.

"Good, then. I will look forward to it. Now I should go speak to your other guests. Is that alright with you, Binny?"

The boy's expression cracked a fraction more, and his little mouth widened just enough to reveal two pearl-like front teeth. "Fine," he said.

Elsie laughed in a kindly way. "You are what my father calls 'a man of few words,' Binny. That can be an admirable trait."

"Come now, Miss Dinsmore," Mrs. Nickle interrupted brightly. "Don't let that boy of mine talk your ear off. I have more guests for you to meet. We are so fortunate here in Lansdale to have such a superfluousness of handsome young men and lovely young ladies."

More introductions were made, and Elsie was surprised that Mrs. Nickle's guests were, without exception, what her father would call "people of quality." The mayor's son was there, and one of the minister's daughters — both of whom Elsie had met previously at her aunt's house.

One young man, whose name was Carter, told Elsie that he had just arrived home from college, and it happened to be the same eastern school that Arthur and Walter attended. As they conversed, Elsie mentioned her two Dinsmore uncles; the young man said he knew Walter well as they were in the same class, though he had never met Arthur.

"I believe Walter is staying at school for the summer session," Mr. Carter said. "He is an excellent student, you know, and a good fellow all around."

"He is," Elsie agreed warmly. Walter and Elsie maintained a regular correspondence, and she was quite proud of how the timorous boy she had known at Roselands had grown into an upright and studious young man. She valued Walter's friendship highly now and was glad of this news of his success in college — Walter being too self-effacing ever to boast about his own achievements.

Overhearing the conversation between Elsie and Mr. Carter, Edgerton turned momentarily pale. Could Carter have seen him around the college? Was there a chance he might be unmasked? If this Carter recognized him, his true identity would quickly come to light, and all his carefully laid plans would be crushed. Edgerton briefly considered excusing himself from the party and retreating to his room. But hiding would only delay discovery, and Edgerton was not inclined to invest more time in a doomed scheme. He decided to risk all. He turned and confronted his possible nemesis.

"How do you do, Mr. Carter?" he said, extending his hand. "I'm afraid Mrs. Nickle forgot to introduce us. I am Bromly Edgerton."

"A pleasure to meet you, Mr. Edgerton," Carter replied. "I believe you are, like Miss Dinsmore, a new arrival in our fair town."

They conversed for some time, and Edgerton detected not a trace of recognition in the young man's tone or manner. His relief was enormous, but he took the incident as another warning. His situation here was by no means safe, and if he were to accomplish his goal, he must move swiftly.

The party was everything Mrs. Nickle hoped. The young people clearly enjoyed themselves. There was much laughter and pleasant conversation; then they played several games including a difficult one called "Stagecoach" at which Lottie excelled. Mrs. Nickle served an excellent fruit punch — "Not a trace of vinegar," Lottie whispered to Elsie when the cups were passed — and a delicious array of cakes, dried fruits, and nuts, which Mrs. Nickle referred to as her "fiddles" instead of "viddles."

As ten o'clock neared, Elsie looked around for little Binny. She spotted him sitting in a corner of the window seat, eating fruitcake and looking as stern as ever as he watched the lively company. "I said I wanted to talk with you before the evening ended, and I must be going soon," she said, taking a place beside him. "What do you think of your mother's party?"

"Fine," he murmured.

"Tell me, Binny, you look to be about six years old. Do you go to school yet, or will you go this fall?"

"Fall," he managed between bites of cake.

"I know you will enjoy school, Binny. It's great fun, I always think, to learn new things every day. Can you read yet?"

He mumbled, "Uh-huh," which Elsie took for "yes."

"Good for you. Reading is my favorite pastime. I'd rather read the Bible than do anything else, but I also like adventure stories and history. What do you like to read?"

Without a blink, the little boy said, "Robin Hood."

Elsie laughed. "So you like adventures as well. That means we have something in common. I must be going now, Binny, but I have enjoyed my conversation with you very much. Perhaps we shall talk again soon."

The boy said nothing, so she stood to walk away. But something halted her. It was a little hand grasping her lacy white skirt. She looked at the child, whose face — freckled like his sister's and dotted with fruitcake crumbs — was lit with a wide grin.

"You are as beautiful as maid Marian, Miss Elsie," he said in an awed whisper.

Instinctively she bent to hug him. "And you, Sir Binny Nickle, are as gallant as Richard the Lionheart."

When Mrs. Nickle's guests had all departed and her children were in bed, she began to clear away the empty plates and cups that lay about the parlor. Edgerton volunteered to assist.

"Well, Mr. E, you escorted Miss Elsie to her door. Do you think she had a good time tonight?" Mrs. Nickle asked hopefully.

"A very good time. She said so herself."

Looking at a plate on which most of a slice of cake remained, Mrs. Nickle shook her head and said, "She wouldn't eat much. Perhaps she doesn't like my cooking."

"But you're wrong, Madam. I have observed that she is very careful about her diet and that she rarely eats anything after supper. You should really be complimented that she partook of your comestibles."

"Com — what?"

"'Fiddles,'" Edgerton smiled.

"I must remember that word. 'Combustibles.' It's a good, long one, and I'm always trying to improve my dictionary."

"A worthy endeavor," Edgerton replied without bothering to correct her.

"You know, Mr. E, I believe Miss Elsie has taken something of a shine to you. I wouldn't say anything to Miss Stanhope, of course, but I do think you have found favor in her niece's beautiful hazel eyes."

Hoping inwardly that his landlady could indeed hold her wagging tongue, Edgerton said only, "I think you misread friendship for favor."

CHAPTER

False Promise

*"Above all else, guard your
heart, for it is the
wellspring of life."*

PROVERBS 4:23

False Promise

*E*lsie was not the only young lady of Lansdale who had formed a favorable impression of Mr. Edgerton. Other girls were attracted to his good looks, courtly manners, and educated conversation, and they were not all above flirting with the newcomer when the opportunity presented itself. Now, no man enjoyed trifling with the affections of women more than he. In truth, Tom Jackson/Bromly Edgerton held women in such low esteem that he cared nothing at all about hurting them and trampling on their virtue. He had left many broken hearts in his wake over the years, and never cast a backward glance.

This was not the time to play the roué, however, and he dared not show any hint of his true character lest Elsie flee from his clutches. So he politely ignored other offers and focused on his prey, becoming more attentive each day. But in the end, it was not his obvious charms that won her heart. It was a serious fault.

Walking in Miss Stanhope's garden on the afternoon after Mrs. Nickle's party, Edgerton was telling Elsie several stories of the hazardous, even life-threatening, adventures he had survived during his travels. One particularly frightening tale involved a mountain climb in Peru when he nearly lost his life, to be rescued at the last possible moment.

Elsie shuddered as he ended his story.

"Did that frighten you?" he asked.

"Not frighten in the way you mean," she said slowly. "But it seems to me a dreadful thing to deliberately risk one's life when no good can come of it."

"If you were man or boy," he said confidently, "you would know that risk is the thrill of all adventure."

"But does that make it right?" she asked.

"It's a matter of taste, I suppose. Or of choice, since one is choosing between the possibility of a long and dull life or a short and exciting one."

Elsie stopped walking and looked full into his face. "Is that really what you believe, Mr. Edgerton?" she asked in a manner that startled him. "If it is, then I am disappointed."

"Why? What have I said to cause this reaction?"

"God gave you your life, Mr. Edgerton, to use in His service — not to toss aside for a momentary excitement. Before throwing His great gift away, you should be very sure of going to a better place."

"But how can anyone be sure there is a better place? Can anyone be sure of anything? How can we know anything beyond question, Miss Dinsmore? Why, I cannot even prove my own existence, can I? There are insane people who believe themselves to be kings or mythical creatures. How do I know that I am not as mistaken in my beliefs as they are in theirs?"

Seeing the look of shock on her face, Edgerton attempted to change the mood. "Pay my ramblings no mind," he coaxed.

"I must, Mr. Edgerton, for I value your friendship."

"Please, Miss Dinsmore, do not mistake me for an infidel."

"But are you a Christian, sir? I believed you to be, but your words indicate otherwise."

Elsie turned and began to walk back to the house. Her head was lowered, and Edgerton could see her shoulders heaving from tears or sighs. For the briefest moment, he felt a pang of fear. Had he ruined his plan with some chance remarks? Then he recalled his conversations with Arthur Dinsmore, and his mood shifted from panic to exaltation. Struggling to keep triumph out of his voice or expression, he ran to catch up with her, taking her arm in his strong hand and turning her toward him.

Elsie saw a beleaguered face and tears misting in his eyes, but she said nothing.

"I — I would be destroyed to lose your respect, Miss Dinsmore," he stammered out. "But you must hear me. I am not a Christian, not a true Christian as you are. But I want to be. Believe me, I have tried to be. It may have sounded as if I were making light of your faith, but nothing could be farther from the truth. If I spoke jokingly of life and death, it was only because until I met you, I was resigned to living out my life as a Christian in name only. And what kind of life is that for a man?"

No one who heard this outpouring could have doubted his sincere anguish. But behind the tear-filled eyes and desperate words, Edgerton's mind was clicking at full speed. He watched Elsie's face, appraising her reaction as coolly as if he were pricing fruit at the market. As he spoke, he saw her expression change — from dismay and regret to surprise to compassion.

"Oh, Miss Dinsmore," he sighed, dropping his hand and hanging his head, "I have all but given up hope for myself. I cannot do it on my own. I am like a wounded soldier in battle. I need help to find my way to a safe place."

Without thinking, Elsie laid her hand on his arm. She remembered her own father's terrible struggle to find his true faith, and with that memory, she understood that her place was not to judge but to lead, if she could.

"Perhaps I have enough hope for us both, Mr. Edgerton. I cannot bear to see you in this dreadful torment of conscience." She began to hold more tightly to him, directing toward a little bench at the back of the garden.

"I will help you all that I can, sir, and gladly," she said.

Reaching the bench, she sat, and he slumped close beside her, burying his face in his hands.

"The answer is much simpler than you think," Elsie said soothingly.

"But what can I do?" Edgerton asked, his voice breaking with feigned emotion.

"'Believe in the Lord Jesus, and you will be saved . . . ,'" she quoted from the Book of Acts. "That is all He requires of you, Mr. Edgerton, that you open your heart and have faith. 'Stop doubting and believe.'"

"But can it be so easy? Mustn't I do something?"

"God shows us the way, sir. The prophet Isaiah has told us, 'Let the wicked forsake his way and the evil man his thoughts. Let him turn to the Lord, and He will have mercy on him, and to our God, for He will freely pardon.' Don't you see, Mr. Edgerton?"

At her question, he raised his head and looked into her eyes. Tears flowed down her pale cheeks, and each one of them was for him.

"You can't think your way to faith," Elsie was saying. "You must open your heart and accept Jesus as your Savior, and let His sacrifice redeem you and His love fill you."

"I am a wicked man," he said.

"Whatever you have done, Jesus has already borne the penalty for you. All He asks in return is your faith and love. And He offers you His righteousness and salvation as a free gift. Can you accept that gift, Mr. Edgerton? Will you?"

Pausing for effect, Edgerton raised his eyes skyward. After some moments, he said in a soft whisper, "I believe that I can, Miss Dinsmore, if you will stand with me and be my guide."

A heavy sigh escaped the girl, and she lowered her head and clasped her hands. "Help us, dear Father, to follow Your perfect path," she prayed.

Edgerton would have pushed his advantage and professed his undying love at that moment, but a door banged loudly from the house, and Phyllis's voice rang out, "Here, you chicks! Phyllis has your supper."

"You should leave now, Mr. Edgerton. Aunt Wealthy will be waking from her nap, and I should go to her," Elsie said, the regret plain in her voice. "But consider what we have said here, and we will talk again later."

"As soon as possible," he replied with urgency, "for I feel as if my head were spinning from your words."

"Not my words," she said with a gentle and — was it possible — loving smile. "If you are spinning, it is from the promise which our Lord has made to you."

And so they parted, both in a state of joy, but for reasons that could not have been more opposed.

~⌒⌒~

Edgerton went directly back to his rented room and with his door closed and locked, he took out pen and paper to write a letter.

Elsie's Stolen Heart

"Art, old man," it began, "the deed is almost done. Do you remember when we discussed allowing your little niece to 'convert' this old sinner? It has turned the trick quite brilliantly. She truly believes that she has rescued me from the brink of eternal condemnation. I must confess there was a moment when I half-believed it myself, for she is most persuasive. But she herself now stands on the brink, and if I do not miss my guess, it won't be long before she and her inheritance are mine. Not a minute too soon. For a man of my tastes, the strait-laced life I have led among the hayseeds of this town is like a prison. I would gladly give girl and money up if I thought I had to go on this way forever. But my escape — and our good fortune — is within sight. Once the knot is tied and the property secured, I will end this charade. She will learn soon enough that her endless talk of religion is over and done with.

"I shall contact you when there is more news. I must endure a little longer. There is a church service tonight where I will see her again. Tomorrow I give myself a rest from all this sweetness and moral rectitude, but I shall return on Friday to hunt the fox to ground."

He signed with his initials — T. J. — addressed the envelope, and hurried out of the house to the post office.

Several days later, the letter was in Arthur Dinsmore's hands. As he read it, his fury mounted. Reaching the initials, he angrily tore the letter to bits and threw them into the empty fireplace grate. What an outrage, Arthur thought. Jackson's audacity infuriated him. Arthur's feelings arose not from any affection for Elsie, though he regretted that even she would be bound for life to so villainous a husband, but from the assault on his family pride. To think that this contemptible scoundrel Jackson was on his way to becoming a member of the Dinsmore family made the boy's blood boil.

Arthur, who could never accept responsibility for his own actions, now blamed Tom Jackson entirely for the scheme and even, in a twist of logic that would have been incomprehensible to anyone else, for his own gambling debts. But he had hoped for some weeks that the plan would fail and that Jackson would somehow disappear from his life.

The letter said otherwise. Arthur was lacking the moral courage to confess the affair to his father or Horace; his only hope now was to dissuade Jackson from continuing. He decided to write a letter and post it that hour. In it, he tried to convince Jackson that the scheme was doomed to failure, for Elsie would never marry anyone without her father's consent. Horace, he said, was bound to search out every detail of Jackson's former life and to reveal his scandalous past. "What my brother will do to you doesn't bear thinking about," Arthur concluded ominously, "and Elsie will die rather than disobey his commands."

When three days later, he received Arthur's letter — carefully addressed to "Bromly Edgerton, Esquire" — Tom Jackson read it and laughed. "I can see your game, you stupid boy," he said to the absent conspirator. "You think I'm not good enough for your precious family. Well, we shall see, little man."

He composed a cautiously worded reply, short and to the point:

"Your warning and advice come too late, old man. However unworthy you and others of your clan deem your humble servant to be, I shall soon become connected by marriage to the illustrious '*D*' family. The girl loves me and believes in me, and I defy all the fathers and relations on earth to keep us apart.

"Do not forget, my friend, that debts of honor are debts for life. You owe me thousands, and I hold your paper. I doubt your family's name and famous pride would be any less damaged by revelation of your debts and your part in this plot. We have a contract, don't forget, which you dare not breach. Say nothing, or suffer the consequences."

This letter was posted that very day and was soon on its way east by fast train.

CHAPTER

A Fateful Encounter

"'Can anyone hide in secret places so that I cannot see him?' declares the Lord."

JEREMIAH 23:24

A Fateful Encounter

The July night was sultry in the river city of Cincinnati, Ohio. In search of a cooling breeze, two gentlemen strolled the gardens of a large estate in a fashionable suburb. The two old friends had not seen one another for several years, so their conversation was mostly of the catching-up sort. But the older man had been silent for some time now, and the younger man sensed that something important occupied his friend's thoughts.

"Your home is beautiful, Beresford. It's good to see you and your family prospering here," the younger man said at last.

"Yes, Edward, we want for nothing these days. But I fear that my wealth is more curse than blessing on my children," Mr. Beresford replied. "At least, on my eldest, Rudolph."

Edward Travilla was caught unaware by the sadness in his friend's voice. "Tell me, if you care to, what troubles the boy."

"Ah, what does not!" Beresford responded in a voice of despair. "I ought not burden you with my problems, but frankly I am at a loss. Rudolph is a likable boy, and intelligent — or so I believed. But he does not seem to understand that wealth is no excuse for idleness. I had looked forward to taking him into my business, but there seems no hope of that now. The truth is that he has fallen into the worst sorts of vices — drinking heavily, gambling, associating with the lowest types of people."

They had come to a patio, and Mr. Beresford leaned heavily against the railing of its carved stone fence. "It's breaking his mother's heart, and mine, for nothing we do seems to help the boy. You should see him, Edward — hardly twenty years old, yet his face already bares the obvious signs of his dissipation. He disappears for days at a time and returns home only for sustenance and more funds to fuel his habits."

"But can you not cut off his money?" Edward asked.

Beresford pounded the hard stone rail with his fist. "No, I can't, thanks to my own foolishness. Thinking I was doing right, I settled a large sum on the boy when he was eighteen. I honestly believed the responsibility would be good for him. Instead he uses the money that I earned to support his gambling and drinking. I might exercise some authority if I were expected to settle his debts, but so far he has not come to me for that purpose."

Edward hardly knew how to advise his distraught friend. "I will help you in any way I can," he said, "but I have no real experience since I am not a father. Yet I know that other good men share your circumstances and that the outcome is not always hopeless. You think you can do nothing for Rudolph, but you can pray for him. Give your troubles to God and trust Him to show you the way."

"You're correct, of course. Your sympathy does me good, Edward, and your words remind me where real power for change lies. I'm a self-made man, as you know, and inclined to trust myself too much. But you are right, my friend. I must have faith that God will bring my boy around, if that is His will."

Edward Travilla was a guest in the Beresford home for three days, and not once in that time did young Rudolph make an appearance. Though Mr. Beresford and his wife made every effort to entertain their guest from the South,

Edward could see the pain that they tried so hard to hide. He might have left their home to ease their suffering, but when he made a suggestion along those lines, Mr. Beresford was adamant that he stay.

It was late in the evening of the third day that Beresford, his face flushed and his hands shaking in agitation, entered Edward's room and asked, "Can you come with me, friend? A man in my employ has only just located Rudolph. He is at one of the worst gambling dens in the city, and my employee seems to think the situation is dangerous. My carriage is waiting to take us there."

"Of course I'll come," Edward said, following his friend's urgent steps.

As the carriage rumbled into the city, down cobbled streets into a district which Edward did not know, Beresford explained, "My employee has been making inquiries about Rudolph for some time now, and a contact of his has arranged our admission to this gambling place. Our entree comes from a low fellow, a professional gambler who has provided a password for us. My employee believes that Rudolph has fallen prey to another gambler — a newcomer — and this new man is taking business from the other. There is a grudge between these two gamblers, and we will benefit from their quarrel."

"Perhaps we should leave the carriage some distance from this gambling den," Edward advised. "We don't want to advertise our arrival."

"Good idea," Beresford said, and he signaled this plan to his driver. The carriage came to a halt in a dark street which must have been near the wharves, for Edward could smell the river when he alighted. Instructing the driver to be alert for their return, the two men walked quickly around a corner and soon found the address they were seeking.

With the password, their entry was effected without delay, and they soon found themselves in a large, smoke-shrouded chamber. The room seemed packed with men at tables, loudly placing bets and shouting at their wins or losses. Waiters moved between the tables carrying trays of glasses filled with wines and liquors. The light was dim, and the noise cacophonous. Beresford looked around but could not discern his son among so many man. "He must be here," the desperate father whispered to Edward. "I must *find* him tonight."

A second later, Edward felt a hand on his shoulder and heard a low, malevolent voice at his ear. "Don't turn round, sir," the voice hissed. "What you seek is at a table in the rear. You should move quickly if you want to save him." Then the hand fell away.

"To the rear," Edward said to his friend. "Hurry!"

The two men pushed their way through the crowd and arrived at the back of the room. At a table, they found their quarry. A man and a boy sat at a small table. Both held cards and two stacks of cards lay on the table between them. The light from a nearby lamp fell strongly on the man, and in an instant, Edward registered every line and curve of that cruelly handsome face.

Beresford's attention was on the other player. "It's he — my son!" the father gasped.

No one heard his exclamation, however, for at that moment, the boy dropped his cards and jumped up, his chair tumbling backwards. Even in the smoke and shadows, his ashen face seemed to radiate a ghostly, white light, and in a high pitch of agony, he cried out, "You've

ruined me! You've taken the last of everything I have, you scoundrel!"

Crazed with fear and loathing, Rudolph Beresford didn't see his own father, but Edward caught a movement of the boy's hand and rushed forward. The boy was just about to put a derringer pistol to his head when Edward grabbed his wrist and twisted it fiercely, causing the small but deadly weapon to fall to the floor. The boy let out a scream so desolate that it brought silence to the entire room, and then he collapsed into his father's arms.

In the confusion that followed, Mr. Beresford and Edward managed to carry the boy's limp body away. They escaped the building and dragged Rudolph to the waiting carriage.

"You saved him, Edward," Beresford said in a voice that betrayed his tears. "Now, we must try to redeem him."

A week later, Edward Travilla reached Lansdale, arriving on the early morning train that had brought Elsie and Horace Dinsmore to the quaint town some two months earlier. Directed by the station master to the Goings' Hotel, Edward engaged a room, enjoyed a satisfying breakfast in the dining room, then retired for a few hours' sleep. It was late morning when he emerged, much refreshed, and inquired from Mr. Goings how to find the home of Miss Wealthy Stanhope.

"Are you a friend of Miss Stanhope's," the hotelier asked suspiciously.

"I have not had the pleasure of meeting her yet," Edward replied politely, for Mr. Goings' question struck him as protective rather than mere curiosity. "I am a friend of her nephew, Horace Dinsmore, Jr., and am here at his request to see that his daughter, who is Miss Stanhope's guest, is well."

Mr. Goings smiled. "Good for you, sir. I met Mr. Dinsmore, and quite a fine gentleman he is. You know, Mr. Travilla, we think very highly of Miss Stanhope, and we've all seen how much pleasure the young lady's visit has brought her this summer. Here, let me write down the directions for you."

Mr. Goings' instructions were crystal-clear, and Edward soon found himself at the open front door of a charming house on a pleasant street. He was about to ring the bell when a familiar face appeared before him. Her look of surprise was followed by the brightest of smiles.

"Mr. Travilla!" Elsie exclaimed. Taking his hand, she pulled him inside. "What a grand surprise!"

"You appear to be blooming in this Ohio setting," he laughed as he let himself be led to the parlor.

"Come in and sit down," she said. "I am so excited to see you. But tell me, how are Papa and Mamma? Papa wrote that you were visiting them at the Cape. And Trip? Is he growing like a weed? Just seeing you makes me homesick for all my loved ones."

"I left them well and missing you greatly. That was about two weeks ago, and I have since been staying with an old friend in Cincinnati. But your father asked me to pay you a visit if I had the time. And I managed to work Lansdale into my hectic schedule," he said with a grin.

Elsie laughed, "So I am an afterthought then."

"Nothing more than that," he teased.

"But I must get Aunt Wealthy. She will be so pleased to meet you."

"Can you delay for a few minutes? I'd like to hear all about your stay here first."

And so they chatted, Elsie telling him about her activities in Lansdale and Edward answering all her questions about her family. A half hour slipped by in what seemed just a few minutes, until their conversation was interrupted by the appearance of Bromly Edgerton, who had taken the liberty of entering without announcing himself.

Edgerton saw the pair before they saw him. He stiffened at the sight of Elsie seated close beside a handsome man, whom Edgerton took to be near himself in age, and conversing with such obvious animation. Thinking the stranger to be a serious rival, Edgerton self-consciously coughed and said, "Excuse me, Miss Dinsmore. I should have rung the bell, but —"

"Never mind that, Mr. Edgerton," Elsie replied gaily. "I want you to meet my old friend from the South, Mr. Edward Travilla —"

She stopped, for Edward, turning to see the new arrival, had risen from his seat and was staring darkly at Edgerton.

"You!" Edward exclaimed. "How dare you enter here?"

Edgerton was stunned. "What did you say, sir? Do you think you know me? By my honor, I have never set eyes on you in my life!"

Edward laughed, a hard sound that Elsie had never heard before. "Honor?" he sneered. "What honor can a scoundrel and a cheat claim?"

"What is the reason for these insults, sir?" Edgerton demanded. In other circumstances, he would have issued

a challenge on the spot, but Elsie's presence restrained him. And he was also in some fear of the stranger and what he might know.

Edward's response was quick and devastating: "My reason is your behavior to a young man of my acquaintance in one of Cincinnati's most infamous gambling dens. You must remember bringing that poor boy to the edge of self-destruction. A week ago tonight, it was. You may not have remarked me in the crowd, but I will never forget your face. It is as permanently etched in my mind as the face of that helpless, stupid boy with a gun to his head."

Elsie gasped and looked to Edgerton. His face at this moment spoke nothing but astonishment.

"You wrong me, sir," Edgerton insisted. "I haven't been in Cincinnati for more than two months, and I know nothing of any gambling dens. But I can see that you are in no mood for fairness, so I will take my leave."

Turning to Elsie, he said in a voice that reeked of supplication, "Miss Dinsmore, you must pardon me. I hope to be given the earliest opportunity to explain this man's accusations and to set your mind completely at rest."

He bowed to her and ignoring Edward, turned on his heel, marching from the house in a storm of indignation.

Edward looked at Elsie whose face was pale with terror and confusion. He dropped down beside her and took her trembling hands in his. "My dear child," he said. "I am sorry to expose you to such a scene, but that man's villainy is so fresh with me, and I could not allow you to be around him for even a second."

Elsie gazed at the hands that held her own. "There must be a mistake, a terrible mistake, Mr. Travilla. Bromly — I

mean, Mr. Edgerton — cannot be this person you believe him to be."

Catching her mistake, Edward said urgently, "Surely this man does not mean something to you, Elsie. Is it possible you care for him?"

"Oh, don't say anything more," Elsie pleaded. "I can't bear it right now. Just go away, and return this afternoon. I'll introduce you to Aunt Wealthy then, but please don't expect me to be cordial right now."

Withdrawing his hands and rising from the couch, Edward said, "I wouldn't think of causing you more grief, Elsie. But I will be back this afternoon, when you have had time to compose yourself. You owe it to yourself to hear the whole of my story. But I warn you, child, not to be misled by any excuses that — that man may offer you. Promise that you will hear me out."

Without raising her head, Elsie replied in a quavering voice, "I would never do less for an old and trusted friend. I promise to listen."

"Good-bye, then," Edward said, though in truth he hated leaving her in this state. "I will return at four o'clock."

With great effort, Elsie managed to pull herself together and join her aunt for dinner. If she was not as talkative as usual, Wealthy didn't seem to notice, for the kind old lady was full of stories about Albert, Thomas, and the chickens — all of which had been into mischief that day.

The meal was barely over when the doorbell rang and Chloe appeared, announcing that Mr. Edgerton was asking to speak with Elsie.

"You go entertain him, dear," Wealthy said. "Much as I enjoy the young man's company, I am more in need of my siesta. You run on now."

Edgerton was in the sitting room, pacing the floor. When Elsie entered, he took her hand and led her to the couch. He then closed the door to all but a crack, and came to sit beside her. At once, he began his defense against Edward Travilla's charges.

His words had been carefully rehearsed in the last hour. He began by assuring Elsie that he had never in his life been guilty of gambling, that he regarded wagering as a crime and a sin. Meekly, he confessed that he had, in his youth, "sewed a few wild oats." He admitted becoming intoxicated on several occasions and confessed to visiting a dance hall or two. But none of these things had he found pleasurable, and all were quickly repented. Surely, he appealed, the failings of youth should not be held against him now.

As to the accusations of the morning, Edgerton repeated that he had never before seen Mr. Travilla nor entered any gambling den in Cincinnati. He had, he said, pondered over Travilla's mistaken impression, and it was only after considerable thought that he realized the probable cause. Edgerton said that he had a cousin who bore the same name and was so much like him in appearance that people often took them for brothers when they were children. This cousin, this other Bromly Edgerton, was a dissolute fellow given to gambling and drinking; it was undoubtedly this rascal — not the Bromly who sat next to Elsie and begged her understanding — who had done the terrible things Mr. Travilla spoke of.

To Elsie's innocent ears, his explanations sounded altogether plausible, and as he went through his tale, her expression grew increasingly relieved. But no more relieved than Edgerton himself, for his story was a fragile web of lies, and he was not sure even Elsie would accept the 'identical but evil cousin' fabrication. But he had counted on her desire to believe in him and her naturally credulous nature.

"Oh, Bromly, I knew that it was all a mistake," Elsie sighed happily.

"Then you are satisfied?" he asked.

"Totally."

"I am so glad, dear one, for I could not bear to lose you. You have become dearer to me than all the world, and I don't believe my life would be worth living without you," he professed with growing passion. Taking her hand, he held it to his cheek. "Will you consent to share this life with me? Will you become my own precious wife?"

Elsie blushed becomingly. She wanted to say yes at that instant. But she lowered her eyes and sighed, "I cannot without my father's permission. And he has made it clear that I am too young to think of marriage. He forbade me even to listen to such proposals."

"When was that?"

"When I was sixteen."

"But, darling girl, you are much older now. Please allow me to write to your father and ask for his consent."

Elsie thought for a moment. "Yes," she said, "that seems agreeable enough. It can do no harm, I suppose."

"Oh, thank you, dearest. A thousand thanks!" Edgerton exclaimed, and he quickly kissed her hand before she withdrew it.

"Now tell me who that Mr. Travilla is and his connection to you," he asked, so Elsie explained her father's long

friendship with Edward and how she valued him like a second father.

"Father? Why, he doesn't look a day over twenty-five," Edgerton said in true amazement.

"He's thirty-four, and two years younger than Papa, though both of them look young enough to be my brothers."

So Travilla was not a rival after all, Edgerton thought, but he could still be a potent enemy. Travilla could not be convinced so easily as the girl, and his close connection to the father made him doubly dangerous. Edgerton needed time to think what course he should follow with the "second father."

He talked with Elsie for a bit longer, assuring her repeatedly of his devoted affection; then he excused himself, saying that he wanted to begin writing his letter to Elsie's father. "It will be the most important letter of my life," he said, "and it must be mailed today."

As four o'clock approached, Elsie found herself increasingly torn by conflicting emotions: her happiness, on the one hand, at loving and being loved by Bromly Edgerton in whose innocence she fully believed. And on the other hand, her fear of Edward Travilla's reaction.

Chloe noticed Elsie's agitation. "Are you feeling quite well?" she asked the girl. "Your cheeks look a might flushed."

"I'm fine, Aunt Chloe. I'm just excited because we have a special guest coming to supper, and you'll never guess who it is."

A Fateful Encounter

"Then suppose you save me the trouble. It isn't Mr. Horace come back, is it?"

"No, but almost as close. It's Mr. Travilla."

Chloe's face was lit by a smile of delight. "Sure enough, I'll be glad to see that man. I guess he's about the truest friend you and your Papa ever had."

Edward was just as happy to see Chloe when he arrived at the house at four. He was gracious to Wealthy, talking with her about his recent travels and taking a tour of her gardens, but betraying nothing of the events of the morning. At supper, Elsie ate little, though she conversed as naturally as she could, and Wealthy noticed nothing amiss. After their meal, Wealthy excused herself; she had promised to visit a sick friend nearby and would be away for an hour or two.

So Edward followed Elsie to the parlor, and they held a grave conversation. Elsie carefully informed him of everything that Edgerton had said, hoping against hope that Edward would be willing to accept the explanation as readily as she had. But he immediately saw the holes in Edgerton's story.

"Dear Elsie, to accept his excuse is to doubt my own eyes. I assure you, child, that I was as close to him as I am to you now. The light was strong on his face, and each line is engraved in my memory. No cousin, if there is one, could look so like him as to be identical."

Then he asked a question. "Do you know where Mr. Edgerton was a week ago this night? If you can vouch for him, I will most certainly revise my opinion."

Elsie had anticipated this, and her eyes filmed with tears. "I did not see him that day, Mr. Travilla, because he went to Kentucky to meet with a business associate. But

that was not out of the ordinary, for he has taken several short business trips during the last few weeks."

"And no one accompanied him, I suppose," Edward said thoughtfully.

"None that I know, " Elsie replied, "but that proves nothing."

Suddenly she turned on her old friend and demanded, "How can you be so uncharitable? You've always been the fairest of men, yet now you're ready to convict an innocent man of a terrible wrong-doing. I never imagined you could be so unjust!"

"But why should you care to protect a man whom you have known for just a few weeks?" Edward asked calmly. "Surely he does not mean so much to you."

Elsie turned from his gaze. "But he might, if Papa permits," she murmured.

His worst fears confirmed by her own words, Edward walked the floor several times while Elsie sat still as stone on the couch.

Finally she looked up at him, genuine fear in her face. "You can't be so cruel as to tell Papa your opinion of Brom — of Mr. Edgerton, can you?"

"It would be cruel to Horace and yourself if I left him in ignorance. But be assured that I will not attempt to bias your father in his judgment. There would be no point in trying, for you well know that your Papa cannot be swayed by the opinions of others. He will make up his own mind based on the facts."

"Against poor Bromly," Elsie burst out in a mixture of grief and rebellion.

"Trust your father, Elsie," Edward said softly. He came to sit at her side. "Trust his love for you and his fairness to

others. And look into your own heart. Even if you doubt my word or your Papa's wisdom, you know there is One in whom you can always trust."

"I will try," Elsie said with a sigh.

She sat quietly for several minutes, struggling to recover her self-control. Edward was just as disinclined to talk, for it hurt him to his marrow to inflict pain on a girl who had been so important to him for so many years.

Elsie finally broke the silence. "What happened to the boy, your friend's son?" she asked. "Did he shoot himself?"

"No, he was prevented," Edward said. Then he told her what had occurred in Cincinnati, leaving out only his own role in saving young Rudolph.

"His story may have a happy ending yet," he concluded. "Rudolph was so shattered by the consequences of his excesses that his parents have a little hope now that he will truly repent. When I last saw him, he was seeking guidance in the Scriptures, and that must be a good sign."

Edward, seeing that Elsie was looking wan and tired — as well she should after so wrenching a day — indicated his intention to take his leave.

"But before I go, I must ask you to do something. I know that you write to Horace every day. Will you tell him what I believe to be the facts about Mr. Edgerton, or shall I?"

Elsie raised imploring eyes and cried, "But I cannot! I just cannot!"

"Then I will relieve you of this painful task and write to him myself. But in respect for what you know to be your father's wishes, you should refrain from any further private conversation with Edgerton until Horace gives you his express permission. Can you do that?"

"If I must."

"Now, cheer up, child. If you care for this person, you can sacrifice a bit for him. Tell me, do you ride every day as you did at The Oaks? Who are your companions?"

"I ride every day the weather is clear, with Lottie King and —" she hesitated, "and Mr. Edgerton."

"Well then, may I join you tomorrow as your escort?"

"It cannot be very pleasant for you," Elsie said, "to be in Mr. Edgerton's company."

"I can endure it, Elsie, to watch over you. I only hope this unhappy situation will not turn you against me. I'm doing only what I believe Horace would do, were he here, but I could not bear to lose the affection of my little friend."

In spite of herself, Elsie smiled at him. "I don't think that's possible, Mr. Travilla. You've always been so good to me, and I could never turn against a true friend."

"I hope that will always be your feeling," Edward said. "Now I must go. Get some rest, child. Tomorrow will be brighter. And please give Miss Stanhope my thanks for a wonderful meal. Good night, now."

Wealthy returned not long after Edward's departure to find Elsie still sitting in the parlor.

"But where is Mr. Vanilla?" the old lady asked cheerfully. "I did so enjoy his company."

Then she saw Elsie's face, which was dry of tears but pale and drawn.

"What has happened, child? Have you received bad news? Are your parents well?" Wealthy asked as she enfolded Elsie in her arms.

"My family are all fine, Aunt Wealthy, but —" Elsie clung close to her aunt, and the whole story poured out.

Wealthy listened in silence until Elsie was finished. Then the lady, stroking her niece's soft hair, said, "I too have faith in Mr. Edgerton and trust that when all is made clear, he will be proved innocent. But you, child, must do as your father would wish and take your burden straight to the Lord. Remember always that He is there to bear your pain. He will see you through this valley of darkness."

Elsie heard the echo of Edward Travilla's words in her aunt's comforting reminder: "Trust in the Lord."

CHAPTER

Hard Evidence

*"'A word was secretly brought
to me, my ears caught
a whisper of it.'"*

Job 4:12

Hard Evidence

*W*alter Dinsmore didn't know what to make of his brother's behavior. For months, Arthur's moods had been as unpredictable as the summer storms — frequent fits of gloom and depression alternating with unnaturally high spirits and gaiety. But of late Arthur's despondency had been unbroken, and Walter was seriously considering writing to his father for help.

Then one night the younger brother was wakened suddenly by a loud shout. He looked across the small bedroom and in the pale, pre-dawn light, he saw Arthur thrashing about on his bed, tossing his covers away and waving his arms wildly. He was muttering incoherently. On going to his aid, Walter quickly discovered that his brother was burning with fever and shaking with chills.

The physician whom Walter summoned early the next morning said that the fever was serious and advised that Arthur would require round-the-clock attention. He promised to arrange for a nurse to come that very afternoon but left Walter in charge until her arrival. He also advised the boy to write immediately to his parents.

All that morning, Walter tended his brother with the most loving care, cooling his hot brow with damp cloths, administering the medicines the doctor had prescribed, holding Arthur so he would not injure himself when the delirium was at its worst. At last, toward noon, Arthur dropped into a shallow sleep, and Walter gathered his writing materials to pen an urgent letter to Roselands. But as he was writing, he heard Arthur murmur a name.

At his brother's bedside, Walter asked softly, "What about Elsie?"

"She'll never have you, Jackson. Horace won't consent." Arthur said in his troubled sleep.

"Jackson?" Walter asked. "What has Jackson to do with Elsie?"

But Arthur had settled into silence, leaving Walter to wonder at the strange comments. He put his letter aside for the moment. Instead he busied himself by straightening the room, trying to clean up Arthur's untidy mess before the nurse arrived.

His brother's clothes were everywhere — draped over a chair, heaped on the dresser — and Walter hurried to put them in their proper places. A fine silk jacket lay like a puddle at the foot of Arthur's bed, and when Walter picked it up, two sheets of paper fluttered to the floor. Retrieving them, Walter instantly recognized the strong, masculine handwriting.

"Jackson!"

Walter had no intention of reading the letter, but the heading caught his eye. "Lansdale, Ohio." He turned to the second page. Instead of a manly signature at the bottom, he saw initials — "T. J./B. E."

His mind raced. "T. J." was clearly Tom Jackson. But what did "B. E." signify? Walter stared at the page until it came to him. In Elsie's most recent correspondence, she had several times mentioned a Mr. Bromly Edgerton. Realization sent a chill down Walter's spine, and he determined to read the letter in its entirety.

The words jumped out at him: "connected by marriage" . . . "the illustrious 'D' family" . . . "debts of honor" . . . "a contract" . . . "suffer the consequences."

One phrase seemed almost to burn his eyes: "The girl loves me and believes in me . . . ."

"It's a conspiracy," Walter said through clenched teeth. "And that lying, cheating sneak Tom Jackson is behind it all. Not only is he scheming against poor Elsie; he's blackmailing Arthur. I cannot let this happen."

Checking that Arthur still slept, Walter seized his pen and began to write rapidly — not to his parents, but to his brother Horace. Where he once would have vacillated, endeavoring to cover up Arthur's complicity, Walter was now decisive and swift. His letter was a model of simplicity — explaining the circumstances and including a copy of the letter from "T. J./B. E."

When his message was addressed and sealed, Walter summoned one of the waiters who worked in the dormitory — a young man who had demonstrated his trustworthiness in the past — and placed the envelope in his hand with several silver coins. "Take this to the post office immediately. It is of the gravest importance, so guard it carefully," Walter instructed. "The money is for the postage and for yourself."

The servant, who had earlier seen the doctor coming and going from the Dinsmores' apartment, assumed that the letter regarded some illness. So from concern for a student rather than promise of reward, he rushed from the building and hurried into town to complete his task.

In the comfortable cottage on the ocean shore of Cape May, Rose Dinsmore was getting her son ready for bed and Horace was working at the desk in his bedroom when John, his valet, arrived with the evening mail.

Horace sorted through the dozen or so letters, quickly finding what he expected — his daily epistle from Elsie — and three more whose return addresses surprised him. Two from Lansdale carried the names Travilla and Edgerton. The third was in his brother Walter's neat hand.

Naturally he opened Elsie's first, but instead of her usual happy sentiments, what he read puzzled and alarmed him. The few hasty sentences entreated him not to be angry. They spoke of her failure to tell him of one to whom she had given her heart and begged forgiveness for letting this one speak to her of love. Finally, she asked him to be fair and not to judge without hearing all sides of the story. But as no names or details were included, Horace was at a loss.

He quickly opened the letter that bore the name of Edgerton, rightly assuming that this would be the one of whom Elsie wrote. The letter seemed proper on its surface, though its contents did little to allay Horace's concerns. The young man introduced himself and proceeded to praise Elsie and to confess his abiding affection for her. Edgerton had carefully avoided referring to Elsie's inheritance; rather he assured that he would support her in all the comfort and luxury to which she was accustomed. He included pious references to Elsie's positive influence over him and her part in showing him the true meaning of Christian love. Indicating that Elsie had acknowledged return of his affection, Edgerton concluded by asking for Mr. Dinsmore's consent to his daughter's marriage.

Horace laid the letter aside and considered. He had dealt with Elsie's suitors before, so by itself this proposal seemed easy enough to handle. But taken with Elsie's strange requests and entreaties, it became a more serious matter. Perhaps Travilla's communication would shed some rational light.

If Horace hoped for comfort from his friend, he did not receive it. And with trembling hand, he at last opened the envelope from Walter. Its contents, and most particularly the copied letter from "T. J./B. E.," confirmed Edward's story and offered evidence that was both convincing and concrete.

When Rose entered the room, Horace was rushing about, grabbing clothes from his bureau and stuffing them into a valise.

"What is it, my love?" she asked in fearful tones. "What has happened? Oh, Horace, is it Elsie? Is she ill or hurt?"

"She is physically well, but her heart and soul are in jeopardy," he replied. Taking the four letters from his desk, he handed them to his wife. "Read these, and you'll understand. I have to find John. We must take the first train we can catch and that means a long horseback ride tonight."

He hurried from the room, and Rose instantly turned her attention to the letters. What she read brought her to the same conclusion as her husband, and when he returned, she was just completing his packing.

Horace took her into his arms and looked into her wise blue eyes. "Do you agree that I must go?" he asked.

"Oh, yes. Immediately," she replied fervently. "These letters tell me that the danger is imminent. Will you travel directly to Lansdale?"

"First I must go to my brothers. Arthur's illness is serious, and though it will add an extra half-day to the journey, I must see that everything is being done for him. Besides, I need all the evidence Walter can supply before I confront this fortune-hunting swine in Lansdale."

Rose said that she would send his trunk on to Ohio, for she had packed only enough for a few days. Then she kissed her husband, and together they said a brief prayer for their beloved daughter's safety.

Early the next morning, Walter was roused from sleep by a knock at his door. Opening it to a well-known face, he fell into his step-brother's embrace.

"How glad I am to see you, Horace!" he exclaimed, ushering his guest into the sitting room where a cot now crowded the furniture. "Excuse the conditions you see, but I have moved in here so that the nurse can give uninterrupted attention to Arthur."

"How is he doing?"

"You know what doctors always say — 'As well as can be expected.' He's not out of danger yet, and he still cannot talk coherently. But his fever is down, and his physician seems quite confident he will pull through. The nurse is wonderfully good with him."

"I'd like to talk with the doctor before I go," Horace said. "My train leaves at noon."

"Then there will be time. The doctor stops in at about ten. But what of Elsie? Do you think she really cares for that rotten scoundrel Jackson?"

"I'm afraid she does," Horace said, taking a chair and dropping wearily into it.

Walter's face flushed with rage. "But you won't allow —" he began.

"Never!" Horace declared. "But I need your help, Walter. You must tell me everything you know about Tom Jackson, and I also need the original of the letter you found."

Walter quickly complied, and together the brothers were able to recreate a nearly complete picture of all that had happened. Sadly, they had to admit that Arthur was deeply involved in the plot against Elsie, yet it was clear from Jackson's letter that Arthur had made some sort of attempt to cancel the plan before real harm was done. As for Jackson, they confirmed that he was the same person as Bromly Edgerton by comparing the handwriting of Edgerton's letter to Horace with that of the original "T. J./B. E." letter. There was no question the writing matched.

"So, he is not as smart as he thinks," Walter said with some satisfaction.

"And he is overly confident," Horace added. "That will make my task somewhat easier."

Arthur's doctor arrived at precisely ten o'clock, and after he had examined his patient, he spoke at length with Horace who was impressed by the man's competence and thoroughness. Horace told the doctor to spare no expense in treating Arthur, hiring extra nurses as needed.

He also had time to take Walter out for an early luncheon, and the boy, who had not left his rooms since Arthur fell ill, was deeply grateful for this gesture. They went together to the train station, where John was waiting with Horace's ticket for the next leg of the journey.

Elsie's Stolen Heart

On the wooden platform, as the train's steam billowed about them, Horace gave his little brother another strong embrace. "You must take care of yourself, Walter," he said. "Arthur is in the best of hands, I am confident, and I don't want to hear that you have become ill. Assuming that all goes well in Lansdale, Elsie will have you to thank for her rescue, my brother. And Travilla will be glad that you found the evidence to prove his experience, too."

He clapped Walter on the back and said in a hearty voice, "You do the Dinsmore name proud, old fellow — a gentleman and a scholar to be sure."

Then Horace bounded up the steps of his train carriage and was gone.

CHAPTER

10

A Dreadful Duty

"I tell you the truth, the man who does not enter the sheep pen by the gate, but climbs in by some other way, is a thief and a robber."

JOHN 10:1

A Dreadful Duty

*T*here was no peaceful sleep for anyone on the night of Edward Travilla's arrival in Lansdale. Not even the most fervent prayers brought rest to troubled hearts. But Bromly Edgerton, who knew nothing of prayer, slept least of all. Awake in his rented room, looking out the window to the house where his coveted prize lay, he plotted his next move.

"I must get her by herself," he whispered to the night air. "But how? That Travilla fellow will be watching her every move, and when he's not around, the old aunt and the nursemaid will be hovering over her. My first chance will come when we ride tomorrow, if I can manage to divert Lottie King in some way. That will have to do. Unless —"

A savage smile curled his lips, and he lay back on his bed. In his twisted brain, he ran over and over the pretty speech he planned to deliver.

The Stanhope household was just coming to life the next morning when Elsie came down the stairs and heard a light tapping at the front door. Opening it, she found Bromly Edgerton waiting there.

"Thank heavens, it's you, my dearest," he said urgently. "Step out on the porch so we may speak."

Elsie hesitated, for she remembered Edward's request that she not converse privately with the young man until she had her father's permission. But she had not made a promise, and for once, she ignored her conscience.

As she came toward him, Edgerton raised his hand as if to caress her face. But Elsie pulled back, and he retreated.

"A thousand pardons," he said, "for I know that we are not truly engaged. But your beauty is such a temptation."

Blushing, Elsie hurried to a seat in a part of the porch that was hidden from public view by a tangle of vines.

Edgerton followed. "I came to ask a favor of my dearest," he began with a smile. "Is it possible that we might ride out alone today? Miss Lottie is delightful company, but I would like to have you to myself for awhile. There is so much we need to discuss about our future together."

"I would enjoy that too, but I'm never allowed to ride without a lady friend or an escort known to my Papa. And even if I were, Mr. Travilla will be with us today. He has asked to be my escort."

Edgerton lowered his head in order to conceal his fury, but Elsie had guessed his reaction.

"Please don't be angry. I agreed not from my own preference," she said soothingly, "but because it is what my Papa would want."

"And your duty to him is so far above your feeling for me?" Edgerton asked, unable to hide his frustration entirely.

"He is my father and entitled to my obedience whether he is present or absent. That is what the Bible teaches us and what my love for him dictates as well."

Edgerton had learned never to argue against Elsie's religious scruples, so he shifted his attack. "Well, I can hardly be cordial to this Travilla after his false accusations against me. If I were not a Christian, I would have called him out to a duel on the spot. Even now, I would not half regret if some accident befell him and kept him from our company."

A Dreadful Duty

Normally, Elsie would have been shocked by so callous a remark, but blinded by affection, she said, "I can understand your anger, Mr. Edgerton, but believe me, Mr. Travilla has the kindest of hearts. When he learns of his mistake, he will be the first to admit his error and make amends."

"Then I must accept him as a riding companion," Edgerton said, rising. "Whether I could ever accept his apology is another matter."

"Won't you stay for breakfast?" Elsie asked quickly, hoping to delay his departure.

"I would like to, my sweet, but I have some business letters to write. I will return in plenty of time for our ride, and not even old Travilla will spoil it for us."

Travilla, of course, did that very thing. On the ride he stuck by Elsie's side like glue. Fuming, Edgerton was left to escort Lottie, but he made the most of a bad situation. Thinking that Lottie might prove a helpful ally, he determined to make her a confidant. He spoke most eloquently to her of his utter devotion to her friend and the unfairness of Travilla's outrageous claims. Trusting his confidences to be genuine, Lottie sympathized with his plight. She agreed that Elsie's dependence on her absent father was extreme for a girl of eighteen, and volunteered to speak up on Edgerton's behalf when she had the opportunity. "But I make no promises that my words will have the desired effect," she added cautiously.

The riding party returned to the Stanhope house just as a wagon was pulling up to the gate.

"That will be my luggage," Edward announced to Elsie, but loudly enough so that Edgerton was sure to hear. "Your aunt has kindly invited me to stay here until Horace returns, so I asked the livery man to deliver my things from the hotel when he retrieved his fine horses."

He dismounted and helped Elsie and Lottie from their saddles. With a curt, dismissive nod in Edgerton's direction, Edward guided the girls through the gate, saying, "Miss Stanhope has invited you, Miss King, to join us for some cool refreshments after our exercise. Please allow me to escort you both inside."

Elsie could do nothing but cast a forlorn glance over her shoulder. Edgerton caught her eyes and smiled back with a look of pained disappointment so dramatic that it would have befitted the greatest of actors. He was acting; he cared nothing for Elsie's feelings save as they served his purpose. What he would have liked at that moment was to throttle Edward Travilla within an inch of his life.

By accepting Wealthy's invitation, Edward could at least keep guard over Elsie. He wanted to forbid any further contact between her and the nefarious Mr. Edgerton, but that was a duty only her father could perform, and Edward's every prayer now included a petition that Horace would arrive soon. In the meantime, it was his duty to serve as Elsie's protector, however much she might resent him.

Edward had, however, enlisted Wealthy on his side. She was not wholly convinced of Edgerton's guilt, for if anyone knew how easily mistakes can be made, it was Wealthy Stanhope. But Edward, whom she had talked with several times now, impressed her as an intelligent and acute witness. She was also growing to like this Southern gentleman quite well, and she sensed that it was not in his character to speak falsely against another or to rush to hasty conclusions.

When the three riders entered the house, Elsie excused herself to go upstairs and change from her riding outfit, and Lottie accompanied her.

"Don't be too long, girls," Wealthy said, "or Mr. Vanilla and I will devour all the lemonade and cookies."

As Chloe helped Elsie into a pretty summer frock and brushed her shining hair into a neat arrangement held off her shoulders with tortoise shell combs, Lottie launched into a spirited defense of Mr. Edgerton.

"You need not make his case to me," Elsie said.

"Then you believe him? You won't give him up, will you?" Lottie asked.

"Yes, I believe in him," Elsie said with feeling. "And I won't give him up — unless my father commands it."

"I wouldn't for anything!" Lottie declared.

With choking voice, Elsie quoted softly the words of Ephesians, "'Children, obey your parents in the Lord, for this is right.' It is God's command."

"But you aren't a child any longer, my friend," Lottie said in frustration.

"I will always be my Papa's child," Elsie replied. "It would break my heart if he were to disown me, which I know he would do if I married without his consent."

"How you do love this Papa of yours!" Lottie proclaimed, throwing her arms up in a gesture of defeat.

"More than anyone in the world."

Chloe said nothing during this exchange, but when the two girls left the room, she sat down on the bed, her back bent and shoulders slumped as if she were burdened with a heavy load. Chloe liked Mr. Edgerton well enough, and she wanted her precious Elsie to be happy. But the nurse-maid, who had been at Elsie's side since the girl's birth, was deeply worried. She knew that young love is often foolish, and she feared that Elsie was making a terrible error; for all her privileges, the girl was not wise in the ways of the world and might easily be tricked by a cunning scalawag, if that's what Edgerton was. Chloe bowed her head and took her worries to the One who knows all. "And please, Lord," she ended her prayer, "try to get Mr. Horace to us just as soon as You can."

Horace didn't know how many prayers rode with him as his train plunged through town and countryside toward Lansdale. His thoughts were all with his daughter and the painful duty that lay ahead of him. At least, he comforted himself, Edward had been there these last five days. Elsie would be safe when her father arrived.

The train stopped at the familiar little depot late on the second day after Horace had departed from Cape May. His servant John was coming on a later train with the luggage Rose had sent after them. Horace thought of hiring a horse, but he decided to walk to his Aunt Wealthy's house, for the train had been cramped and uncomfortable and he needed to clear his mind and renew his energy with exercise.

Reaching the house, he saw that the front door was open, and he walked in just as Wealthy was bustling about the parlor, plumping pillows and dusting her cherished

family relics. At the sight of her nephew, the little lady rushed to embrace him.

"Dear Horace, I am so glad you've arrived. Elsie is in her room. Go to her now. She needs you."

Horace began to climb the stairs, but he had not taken two steps when the voice he loved so well rang out.

"Papa! Oh, Papa!"

In an instant she was in his arms, clinging to him as she had done when she was a child. He held her close and could feel her trembling. Taking her hand he led his daughter into the sitting room, and Wealthy quietly closed the door upon their reunion.

Gently, Horace directed Elsie to the couch and pulled up one of Wealthy's funny old chairs for himself. Taking Elsie's hand, he looked into her face and was struck by the shadows that encircled her eyes.

"Elsie, dearest," he began, keeping his voice steady and calm, "I am here to put an end to this terrible affair. You know that I would do everything in my power not to hurt you, but this person will hurt you more than anything I can do. You must give him up, for he will destroy your life if you do not."

Tears were rolling down her cheeks. "You'd never ask me to if you knew how much I — I love him!" she protested.

"Hush now. I know what you do not. He is a vile creature — a drinker and a gambler, a swindler and worse. I know these things for fact, Elsie."

"It's not true, Papa!" Elsie cried. "He has been wrongly accused. Mr. Travilla has made a mistake."

"No, Elsie, Travilla is not wrong. I have evidence that confirms Edward's accusation."

"But you must hear Mr. Edgerton's side of the story, Papa," Elsie said, and she repeated to her father all that Edgerton had told her.

"That is his story," Horace commented flatly when she had finished. "But let me show you the proof."

He withdrew two letters from his coat pocket — the one Edgerton had written to himself and the one from Tom Jackson to Arthur.

"Do you not see that the writing is the same? That this man you know as Edgerton is your uncle Arthur's gambling partner and conspirator in this scheme against you and your fortune? I have visited my brothers, and though Arthur is too ill to confess his part in this, the proof is strong and clear. These letters confirm it, Walter confirms it, and even Arthur's fevered words confirm it."

Elsie had turned very pale as she studied the letters. "But this is not proof, Papa. Surely these letters are the work of the cousin. Mr. Edgerton said his cousin was a gambler and a rake. He's obviously a forger as well, and impersonating poor Bromly for some reason."

"Elsie, you are not using your common sense," Horace said with all the old sternness in his voice. "This cousin is a fantasy created to deceive you. Your Edgerton is Tom Jackson, a notorious man who is in league with Arthur to steal your fortune and ruin your life. You must give him up now and give him up forever!"

Elsie was so shaken that she felt she might faint. But the sound of steps on the porch and a voice she knew well startled her.

"Is that him?" Horace asked.

"Yes, Papa," she replied in a hoarse whisper "May I see him — just a few words — in your presence. Please, Papa."

A Dreadful Duty

"No, Elsie," he said firmly. "You are never to communicate with him in any way again. I positively forbid it. You are never to have contact of any sort with this scoundrel again. Stay just where you are, and I will tend to him."

Swiftly, Horace left the room, closing the door tightly behind him. Elsie fell back against the cushions. It seemed that she could not move, as if she had been struck a paralyzing blow. But a few moments passed, and the voices of her father and her suitor drifted through the open window. She rose and went to listen, trying to hear their words and hoping that her suitor could convince her father. She could not clearly understand what was said, but the tone was plain: Horace, cold and controlled; Edgerton, persuasive at first, then loud and full of defiant anger.

It was over in what seemed like an instant. She heard Edgerton's steps retreating down the gravel path, the gate slamming shut, the front door closing.

When Horace re-entered the sitting room, his daughter stood before him, and the look on her face and set of her posture could not have presented a more tragic sight. Her devastation nearly broke his heart, and for a fraction of a moment, he was tempted to relent. But now that he had confronted Edgerton, he was positive of the man's evil nature and vicious schemes.

He went to Elsie and held her tenderly, stroking her hair and soothing, "I know how this hurts you. I would bear all your pain myself if it were possible. I understand that you doubt the rightness of my actions. But Elsie, if you cannot trust me now, turn to Him whom you have always trusted. Go to Him who is your rock and your fortress, and take your refuge in Him. We have been through painful times before, my child, and with His help, we will come through this."

Elsie grew more calm as he spoke, though she clung to him still. After several minutes of silence, she looked up into his face, hugged him quickly, and withdrew from his arms. Turning away, she ran to her room.

Horace did not pursue her. He had done what had to be done, and now Elsie must find her comfort in a higher power.

Horace was suddenly exhausted. He dropped down onto the couch and covered his eyes with his hands. He was sitting in this dejected pose when he heard the swish of silk a few moments later. A small hand rested on his shoulder.

"You are tired, nephew," Wealthy said. "You must eat something and then rest."

Horace looked up and smiled gratefully.

"It is more difficult than I can describe to hurt one's own child in order to save her. But I've been forced into it by that monster, and it is another crime for which I hold him to account."

"Then you are sure he is guilty as accused?" Wealthy asked.

"Yes, dear Aunt," he said, a wan smile coming to his lips. "I am as certain of his treachery as I am of your goodness."

"And are you just as certain that Elsie will obey you?"

"It will be hard on her," Horace said, looking toward the door through which his grieving daughter had passed. "I am not insensible to her age or to the rebellion that strikes every young person as they approach their adulthood. She is not a child, I know that. And were she to abandon me,

she is not without resources. But even if she were inclined to disobey me, her faith and trust in our Heavenly Father is unshakable. In that I have absolute confidence. She will die before she will break faith with her Lord. She will obey me because that is God's command, and His command will keep her from destruction."

CHAPTER

11

Vengeful Pursuits

"Because the Lord revealed their plot to me, I knew it, for at that time he showed me what they were doing. I had been like a gentle lamb led to the slaughter; I did not realize that they had plotted against me . . . ."

JEREMIAH 11:18-19

His confrontation with Horace Dinsmore left Edgerton in a white heat of rage. The accusations Horace had frankly spoken were all true, of course. And the proofs produced were undeniable. Edgerton had tried his lies, but the father was as cynical as the daughter was gullible. In the end, Edgerton was reduced to ranting and sputtering like a thwarted child.

An ordinary man caught so effectively in his falsehoods might have taken at least some of what he heard to heart, felt a modicum of guilt, and contemplated some change in his ways. But Tom Jackson, as he was now revealed to be, was not an ordinary man. What he had of a heart was so dark and stony that no arrow of truth or conscience could pierce it.

He gave not a moment's thought to Elsie. Aside from her physical beauty, she had never held any attraction for him. Her Christian heart and guileless purity repelled him just as pure water repels oil, so that losing her meant nothing to him. In the first stage of his rage, not even her fortune was regretted.

Had he been as smart as he thought himself to be, Jackson would have ended his game at that moment. His losses were redeemable, for there was still Arthur to threaten and squeeze for money. That claim alone could line Jackson's pockets handsomely with Dinsmore coin.

No. What tore at him was the humiliation of being so thoroughly chastened and then dismissed by an honest man. Horace's cold and haughty demeanor had twisted the knife to its hilt. Who did these Southerners think they were, Jackson asked himself again and again. How dare they set themselves above him and treat him as no better than the dirt stuck on their shoes? He hated these uppity men — Dinsmore and Travilla, just like that rich, old Beresford — who thought they were his betters only because they had money and power. But he would have his day. He could bring them to regret their arrogance, and he knew how to do it. These men hurt most when their children hurt.

All these thoughts and many more of the same ilk ran through Jackson's head that afternoon. He had been too angry to go back to his room and face Mrs. Nickle's prying eyes, so he nursed his wounds by walking the hills outside the town until well past dark. Gradually his anger subsided, and his sense of aggrievement grew. He conceived a burning hatred for Horace that overcame all other considerations. "If that man believes this business is ended, he is sadly mistaken," Jackson said to himself. "I will have my revenge, however long it takes. I will take from him that which he values most and break his heart in the process."

By the time Tom Jackson finally crept into Mrs. Nickle's house that night, he was tired and hungry, but elated. He had become Bromly Edgerton again and would not shed that identity until Elsie had surrendered to him.

~

Edgerton's first fear, that the Dinsmores would leave Lansdale immediately, was allayed the next morning at breakfast. According to Mrs. Nickle who had heard it from Willy who got it from Phyllis when borrowing a cup of buttermilk, the Dinsmores were to stay on for another four days, until Monday. So there would be time, Edgerton thought triumphantly.

An hour later, he was carefully making his way by a circuitous route to Wealthy Stanhope's vegetable garden which lay at the back of her property out of sight from the house. Young Simon was there as usual at this time of day, picking fresh vegetables for the dinner table. As the boy came close to the place where Edgerton had stationed himself, the man attracted his attention with a low whistle.

"What you doing in the bushes?" Simon asked.

"I have something for you," Edgerton whispered. "Come here."

The boy saw two glittering objects in the man's outstretched hand. He approached, and the objects became gold coins.

"Those for me?" Simon asked incredulously.

"If you will do me a small favor," Edgerton said. "There is something I would like you to deliver to Miss Dinsmore. A letter. It is for her hand only, and you must be absolutely certain that no one sees you give it to her. Is that clear? No one is to know but Miss Dinsmore herself."

"I can do that easy," Simon said confidently.

"Good," said Edgerton, reaching into his pocket for a small, white envelope. Giving it and one of the gold pieces to the boy, Edgerton said, "This five-dollar piece is yours now. If you achieve your goal without being observed, you will have the other coin."

"Thank you, sir. You can count on me."

Edgerton went back to his room to await the outcome of his scheme. Simon, who knew nothing of Horace's

orders to Elsie regarding Edgerton, assumed that the letter was some little joke, and he watched carefully for his opportunity to complete his assignment. His chance came that afternoon, when the Dinsmores, Edward, and Lottie returned from their ride. Simon was holding Elsie's horse as Horace helped his daughter to dismount. When Horace was distracted for a few moments by his own frisky steed, Simon quickly slipped the envelope into Elsie's hand. The girl looked at it and then at Simon. The boy answered with a broad grin.

Hiding the envelope within the folds of her riding skirt, Elsie walked hurriedly into the house and went straight to her bedroom. Chloe would be coming at any minute, so Elsie had to decide what course to take. How she wanted to open the envelope and devour its contents. It might be more evidence of her Bromly's innocence, and surely she must present such proof to her Papa. But to read it would be direct disobedience of her father. What was she to do?

As she wrestled with her conscience, a tapping at the door brought her debate to an end. Horace entered, and he instantly caught the troubled look in Elsie's face.

"What is the matter, dearest?" he asked, thinking she may have become overheated during their ride.

Elsie didn't reply but simply held the unopened envelope out to him.

Horace's face darkened at the sight of the writing on the envelope's face — a hand he had become all too familiar with in recent days. He turned it over, and was relieved to see that the seal was unbroken.

In a choking voice, Elsie spoke at last: "Shouldn't you read it, Papa? It might contain information to Mr. Edgerton's credit. Oh, please read it, Papa, or allow me to."

"No, Daughter," Horace said in a firm but not unkindly tone. "This person knows that I have forbidden all communication with you, yet he tries to go around me and contact you in secret. That is proof enough of his motives. We need not read his words."

Horace moved to Elsie's little writing table and taking up a pen, he made a few swift marks on the envelope. As he wrote, he inquired, "How did you get this letter?"

Elsie hesitated, for she didn't want to cause trouble for Wealthy's young servant, but under Horace's unwavering gaze, she admitted, "From Simon, Papa. He gave it to me when we came in from our ride just now. But he meant no harm, I'm sure. He has no knowledge of your command."

"Don't worry, dear. I won't hold him to blame, though I shall instruct him to avoid this person in the future."

Chloe came through the door at that point and was immediately alert to the tension in the room.

"I've come to help you change, Miss Elsie," the nursemaid said. "Miss Stanhope says she has some refreshments ready for you down in the parlor, Mr. Horace."

Horace responded by handing over the envelope. "Before you do anything else, Chloe, I want you to take this straightway to Mr. Edgerton. There is no other message, and you need say nothing to him. Just hand the envelope over at the door and come back here."

Chloe had already guessed the source of the letter, and even though the sorrowful look in Elsie's eyes tugged at her loyal heart, the nursemaid was more than happy to carry out her mission.

A few minutes later, Edgerton watched from his window as Chloe bustled across the street. Smiling to himself, he assumed that she was bearing a reply from her mistress —

a quick note probably, to name a time and place for the clandestine lovers' meeting he had requested in his letter. With absolute conviction that his scheme had succeeded, he listened for Chloe's steps on the porch, heard the front door open and a few words spoken by Willy, and waited for delivery of Elsie's response.

What Willy handed to him was his own letter — Elsie's name crossed out with bold slashes and his own name inserted by a heavy hand. Shutting his door to Willy, he stormed across his room, crushing the envelope in his fist and hurling it to the floor. From his window, he glowered at the house across the street, focusing on the window behind which he knew Elsie resided.

"You stupid girl," he hissed under his breath. "You stupid, stupid girl."

The misdirection of his letter was only a temporary set-back in Edgerton's plans. There was another avenue to his objective, and he took it that evening by calling on Lottie King.

Seated in the Kings' parlor, he unwound a pitiful tale for her, repeating his claims of innocence and telling her of the incident of the letter.

"I know it was wrong of me to send it in secret," he said with bowed head, "but I am desperate for word of her. I will not rest until I know she has not been turned against me."

"I am certain she has not," Lottie said with sympathy. "But I am just as sure that she gave the letter to her father, for she will not disobey him."

"Does she really have so little sense?" he asked.

"She has a great deal of sense," Lottie replied a little stiffly, "but she is conscientious in her duty to her father and will obey his commands though doing so may be breaking her heart."

"Please help me, Miss Lottie," Edgerton beseeched, and Lottie was not immune to his appeal.

"But what can I do, Mr. Edgerton?"

"Go to her on my behalf. Arrange for her to meet with me in privacy. I only want a few moments alone to —"

Lottie suddenly stood up. "That I will not do, sir. I would never tempt Elsie to violate her conscience in that way. You forget that I'm her friend and have the utmost respect for her."

Edgerton tried again, pleading his case with all the eloquence he could summon. But Lottie was unmoved. His request had revealed a fault in his character that she had not perceived before.

The girl at last interrupted his pleading and said, "I think it is time you go, Mr. Edgerton. Excuse me." At that, she strode from the room, leaving Edgerton no choice but to depart in anger and frustration.

He had some hope that Lottie would not reveal this interview to Elsie, but Lottie felt no further obligation to keep his confidences. As early as she could the next morning, she went next-door and sought Elsie out. In the quiet of Elsie's room, Lottie revealed the whole of what had passed between her and Edgerton. She did not elaborate or embroider, but told the story straightforwardly.

"He is very desperate," Elsie said, wringing her hands.

"He is," Lottie agreed. "But I think you should consider that the reasons for his desperation may not be what you believe. Perhaps it is not my place to judge, but you must see that his request was not the action of a gentleman."

Elsie looked at her friend in shock. "Have you turned against him too?" she asked as tears welled in her eyes. "Do you believe that my heart is so wrong in loving him?"

Lottie's natural sympathy overwhelmed her, and she took her friend in her arms. "Oh, no, Elsie. Perhaps you're right after all, and his actions can be excused as those of a man deeply in love. Don't give up hope that he may someday prove himself to be innocent. So long as you believe in him, there's always hope."

Lottie comforted her friend for some time, but when she left, she was in a state of unease. She had no doubts that Elsie's feelings for Edgerton were pure and honest. But however hard she tried, Lottie could not shake her growing doubts about Bromly Edgerton.

With Horace and Edward guarding her constantly, it was virtually impossible now for Edgerton to contact Elsie. But he tried nonetheless, with a persistence that was obsessive. When they all went for a walk that afternoon, he dogged their steps, not speaking but following their progress at an uncomfortably close distance. That evening he took up his post at Mrs. Nickle's front gate and watched the Stanhope house until the last light was out.

The next morning — the Sabbath — he again followed the group as they walked to church, and he took his seat in a pew across the aisle and just ahead of the Stanhope row. Throughout the service, Edgerton made no effort to conceal his interest, repeatedly turning and staring at Elsie — to the discomfort of other worshippers.

When the service ended, Edgerton rushed away and seemed to be giving up his pursuit at last. Elsie, Horace, Wealthy, and Edward had remained at the church to chat with the minister and several other friends about the day's sermon. Though Horace and Edward both searched for signs of the persistent suitor, Edgerton was nowhere to be seen as they began the pleasant stroll home. But turning the corner onto Wealthy's street, they found themselves face-to-face with Edgerton who was walking with deter-mination toward them.

What terrible effort it cost poor Elsie to look away from him, but that was her father's instant command. Even so, Edgerton strode boldly forward, and when he was nearly upon them, he lifted his hat and said in a loud, cordial tone, "Good morning, Miss Dinsmore."

Elsie tightened her grip on her father's arm, but said nothing. Horace answered for her, his voice low and cold as winter ice: "My daughter acknowledges no acquain-tance with you, sir." He guided Elsie rapidly away, while Edward stayed beside Wealthy, accommodating her slower pace.

"Well!" declared the old lady in her chirping voice after Edgerton was well gone. "I know that he has been revealed as a liar and a forger, Mr. Vanilla. And now we have posi-tive proof of worse. Mr. Edgerton is *no* gentleman!"

CHAPTER

12

Farewells and Homecomings

*"Trust in the Lord with all your
heart and lean not on your
own understanding . . . ."*
PROVERBS 3:5

ear child, this house won't be the same without you," Wealthy sighed, warmly clasping Elsie in her arms. "Horace, you must promise to bring my great-niece back soon, and yourself, and your wife and little boy. And you, Mr. Vanilla — you are invited anytime whether with Horace or on your own. But don't come alone; bring your mother, for she sounds just the sort of lady I should like."

Everyone was crowded onto the porch, saying their farewells.

"Even if you come in a bundle, you have seen that my home and our town can accommodate one and all, and everyone welcome," Wealthy laughed.

Then turning to Elsie and hugging her once more, Wealthy added, "Despite the end of it, my dear, this summer has been a wonderful beginning, for you have brought me all the joys of being a grandmother without the bother of being a mother. I shall miss you with all my heart, dearest."

"As I will miss you just the same, Auntie," Elsie said in a hoarse little whisper.

Lottie, who was standing nearby with her sister, said gaily, "Let her go now, Aunt Wealthy, or they will miss their train. Though I am not Elsie, I offer myself in her place whenever you need someone to hug."

"And I will accept your offer, Lottie dear," Wealthy said. "Now, off you go, all of you, for your carriage is waiting at the depot and your train is at the gate!"

Even Elsie laughed at this remark, and Wealthy apologized for "putting the horse before the cart again."

With one more round of farewells, Elsie, Horace, and Edward went to the carriage and got in, but as the horse began to pull away, they heard a voice shouting excitedly. It was Mrs. Nickle with Willy and Binny.

"Good-bye, Miss Dinsmore!" Mrs. Nickle cried. "Have a *commodious* journey!"

"Bye, pretty lady," Binny said with a pretty little smile.

Willy waved but said nothing. And Elsie waved in return.

Chloe and John had arrived at the depot earlier, so the baggage was all checked and loaded. The train was only a few minutes from departure when Elsie and her stalwart guardians stepped onto the platform. She didn't even see the tall, darkly handsome figure who waited there, but Horace and Edward noted Edgerton's presence immediately. They hurried Elsie aboard, and Horace led his daughter to a comfortable compartment while Edward returned to the platform for a last-minute word with the servants. Seeing Elsie to her seat, Horace quickly closed the curtain of the carriage window.

"But, Papa, I should like a last view of Lansdale as the train leaves," Elsie said.

"When the train is out of the station," Horace replied evenly, "and the steam has cleared, I'll open the curtains again."

The figure on the platform cursed as the train wheels began their slow, grinding revolutions. A bell was rung, a whistle was blown, and his victim departed without a backwards look. Edgerton hadn't expected to speak to Elsie, knowing that her father would prevent even a single parting word. But he had fervently wanted the girl to see his face, so full of longing and love, one more time.

He had wanted his countenance imprinted upon her mind.

"Oh, well," he said to himself, "I will see you again soon enough, my silly little heiress. And when I do, we will know if all the fathers in the world can keep me from having my way." Then he laughed, loudly and long, as he walked the dusty small town streets back to his boarding house and his own packing.

The return to the midst of her family was, both Horace and Rose hoped, the beginning of their daughter's healing from her first, disastrous encounter with romantic love. Rose saw immediately how thin and pale her daughter had become, but the Cape was a perfect place to regain and renew strength, both physical and spiritual. The weather was warm and sunny, the sea air bracing, and the company could not have been better.

The Allisons had rented a cottage on a property that adjoined the Dinsmores', and all of Rose's brothers and sisters were present, excepting Edward who remained in Philadelphia to tend to the family business. The young Allisons were a merry and carefree group who engaged in every activity the seashore community offered — picnics and bathing in the surf, campfire suppers on the beach, horseback rides and long, rambling walks, excursions to sites of interest. They included Elsie in everything they did, and although she was at first reluctant to participate, with Horace and Rose's urging she soon found herself looking forward to days full of fun.

Elsie's Stolen Heart

Sophie Allison had always been her special friend, for they were almost the same in age, and it was not long before Elsie confided in Sophie about Bromly Edgerton and what had occurred in the previous months in Ohio.

"Do you still love him?" Sophie asked one afternoon as she and Elsie walked alone by the shore, searching for interesting seashells and watching as storm clouds gathered far out over the ocean.

"I know that I shouldn't, but I do," Elsie admitted. "Despite what Papa and Mr. Travilla say, I am certain they are mistaken, and that Bromly is a man of fine character."

"Then perhaps hope is not lost for you," Sophie said brightly. "If the gentleman can prove he is not what your Papa thinks, then I know Uncle Horace will back down from his position."

"That is what I long for," Elsie sighed.

"When we first met, I thought your father was excessively strict with you. Remember how he wouldn't allow us to talk after we had said our prayers and gotten into bed. I used to bite my knuckle raw to keep silent."

Elsie laughed, "You didn't!"

"I did. You know what a chatterbox I was. I always had just one more thing to say."

Elsie put her arm around her friend's waist, and they walked together as they did as children, giggling and laughing at memories of the adventures they had enjoyed together.

After some time, Sophie returned to her original subject. "I know that this summer has been very hard for you, Elsie. Do you feel very angry with your Papa?"

Elsie nodded and replied, "I have felt so at times, Sophie — angry and rebellious at what seems so unjust. But I know that Papa is much wiser in these matters than I am and that he would never do what he believes is wrong. I *want* to be obedient to him, Sophie, and I am. But I often feel as I did when I was a little girl — impatient to have my way."

"Patience is so difficult at our age," Sophie said wisely. "We wait to be grown-up for so many years, and now that we are almost there, it's difficult not to want all the privileges of being an adult. I look at my friends who are already married and setting up their own homes, and I want to be like them. Sometimes I feel frightfully jealous of them. But Rose told me something this summer that has helped me very much. We were talking about love and marriage, and she said that love is not a thing that can be manufactured out of wishes. She said that those who look for love have the hardest time finding it and are likely to be mistaken in their choices."

"Do you think I may be mistaken?" Elsie asked.

"I can't say. I know that you believe in your Bromly, yet I also know that your father has a great deal of evidence against him. Is it possible that Uncle Horace is right about him? Could it be your pride and impatience rather than true love that makes you cling to your faith in the man's innocence?"

Elsie was silent, and Sophie feared that she had said too much. She never wanted to hurt her friend.

"There may be something in what you say," Elsie responded at last, her words coming slowly and without any sign of rancor. "I've been so upset that I haven't been able to think clearly about my feelings."

"Well, then you are wise to follow your Papa's commands until the issue is resolved. And to take your problems to our Beloved Savior, your Heavenly Friend."

"I do, Sophie, and He is my greatest comfort. He calms my anger and soothes my pain as no earthly friend can do. Isn't it wondrous to have One who accepts us and loves us in all our troubles?"

"He is our refuge and our fortress," Sophie said softly.

The two walked on for a bit until they noticed that the dark clouds, which had been far out at sea, were rolling toward the shore. So they turned and retraced their steps to their houses. The sky was nearly black, and large raindrops were falling when Elsie reached the steps to the Dinsmore cottage, but the lights inside beckoned her in, promising warmth and shelter from the storm that was breaking.

~~~

The Dinsmores and the Allisons left the Cape late in September. Autumn was just beginning to brush the South with her rich colors when Horace and his family arrived back at The Oaks. Harvesting was underway, and great stacks of hay and corn stalks stood in the fields like sentries at arms, on guard to greet the family. The gardens were aglow with fall blooms against the deep, dusty green of trees and bushes that would soon turn crimson and gold. The estate house fairly sparkled, for the servants had polished it inside and out, top to bottom, in anticipation of the homecoming. Elsie had never been so glad to see The Oaks.

Farewells and Homecomings

Within a few days, life settled into its comfortable routines. Horace was often away with his plantation manager, overseeing the harvest and preparations for winter planting. Elsie, who no longer had formal studies herself, now helped with little Trip's schooling and took him on pony rides in the afternoon. She also assisted Rose who had brought two trunks filled with the latest fabrics and patterns back from the North and was furiously sewing winter fashions for everyone. Adelaide Dinsmore was a frequent visitor to The Oaks, as was Edward Travilla. Enna Dinsmore, as pert and catty as ever, also made her appearances, which Horace joked were more like royal visitations.

The summer seemed to drift farther and farther away until one morning at breakfast when Horace was sorting the daily mail. Everyone received something — several letters to Rose, a note to Trip from his grandmother Allison, and two envelopes addressed to Elsie. Horace handed her the first, which was from Sophie, but held back the second.

"Elsie, dear," he said, looking questioningly at the face of the envelope, "I do not recognize this writing, and the return address is unknown to me. Can you make out the postmark?"

She took the letter and gazed at it. "It's smudged, Papa, but it doesn't look familiar."

"Well, finish your breakfast first, and then you can read it."

Elsie did as instructed, though her curiosity had been stirred by the strange handwriting. She ate well, for her appetite was fully restored now, chatted with her parents about the day's plans, and teased with Trip. At length Rose finished her meal and excused herself, taking Trip away for a thorough hand and face washing. Elsie was about to rise when her father said, "Stay dear, and open your letter here. But I want you to check the name of the sender first. Don't read the contents until you have ascertained the author."

Surprised by her father's command, she looked at him and saw that his expression had grown dark and serious. Wondering what troubled him so (for she supposed the letter to be from one or another of the young people she had met at the Cape), she quickly broke open the envelope and removed several sheets. Turning to the last page, she saw the name; instantly her face flushed, and her hand began to shake.

She looked to her father and saw his outstretched hand.

"Please let me read it, Papa," she pleaded.

"No," he said, his voice low and hard with anger. "Hand it to me."

She did as she was told, but tears were falling from her eyes.

Horace then turned to the signature, and as soon as he saw the name, he folded up the sheets, returned them to the envelope, and put it into his coat pocket.

"This is not worthy of a single tear or regret," he said coldly. "I will return it at once." Then his voice softened: "Unless you prefer that I read it first."

Her head lowered to hide her tears, Elsie replied, "No, Papa."

"Do you not see now, child, that this man is fully able to disguise his handwriting as he wishes?"

"But that doesn't mean he has done so before, Papa."

"So you think he has behaved correctly to subvert my command by writing you and hiding his identity in this way?"

"He's not perfect, Papa, but I can't believe he is as bad as you think."

"How can you be so blind?" Horace exclaimed in vexation. "I will take care of this. You are excused now."

Elsie, her tears now uncontrollable, whispered a choked "Yes, Papa," and dashed from the room.

Rose, who had come to the door in time to observe this scene, let Elsie pass and came to her husband's side, putting a loving hand on his shoulder.

"I thought this thing was over," he said roughly. "I thought the fellow would have moved on to another poor victim by now."

"But do not blame Elsie for his sins, dearest," Rose said. "She is suffering so much."

"It's her own fault! She refuses to see what is plain before her face. My hearts bleeds for her, Rose, but she willfully refuses to acknowledge the truth. I am afraid my patience is wearing very thin."

"There must be some truth she will accept, my dear," Rose said. She moved to her chair and sat beside her husband. "I have been wondering about something. How did Mr. Edgerton come to know Elsie in the first place?"

Horace, who was in no mood to discuss Bromly Edgerton at length, shrugged and replied shortly, "Arthur arranged some kind of introduction for him to Aunt Wealthy. I was never able to get the details out of my brother. After he recovered from that fever, he shut up like a clam and denied all knowledge of Edgerton or Tom Jackson or the plot against Elsie."

Rose went on calmly, ignoring her husband's temper. "Elsie may think she is in love, and all girls in love will protect the objects of their affection. But your daughter is no fool, Horace. She will not deny the undeniable. Might it not be worthwhile to investigate the nature of Bromly Edgerton's introduction to your aunt?"

Horace looked into his wife's gentle face, and a smile came to his lips. "You are brilliant, my dear. If it can be proved that the scoundrel's actions were fraudulent from the outset, Elsie will have to face the truth. Arthur will tell me nothing, of course, but I never questioned Aunt Wealthy about how Edgerton came into her home. I was too much concerned with getting my child away from him."

He reached across the white tablecloth and took Rose's hand in his. "You are thinking more clearly than I, darling wife, and I thank you. Will you excuse me now? Perhaps you can talk to Elsie and tell her that my anger is not directed at her. I must write a letter to Lansdale."

Several weeks passed, and no more attempts at contact were made by Elsie's thwarted suitor. She had gone through some difficult days after the arrival of the letter, but with Rose and Horace's sympathy and encourage- ment, she had recovered her normal pleasant nature (although in private her thoughts still went to her Bromly and her hope that he would someday acquit himself in her father's eyes).

An invitation had come from her old friend Lucy Carrington to visit for a few days at Ashlands. There had been something of an estrangement between the two families after Herbert Carrington's death. It was by

no means a bitter break, but there had naturally been some distance, given Horace's actions in refusing to consent to Herbert's request for Elsie's hand. The Carringtons did not blame Horace for precipitating Herbert's final illness, for the boy had been sick for many years, but the incident had caused discomfort on both sides.

Lucy's invitation offered the opportunity for everyone to put aside past feelings and repair old friendships. Besides, Elsie had not been away from The Oaks since their return from the North, and Horace and Rose both agreed that a visit with Lucy would be good for their daughter.

Autumn was well established on the morning Elsie mounted her horse, Glossy, and with Jim as her escort, rode to Ashlands. Chloe was to follow with the luggage required for a five-day visit.

Lucy was in the highest spirits when she met her friend in the driveway. Mrs. Carrington followed at her heels, and the kind lady seized Elsie in an embrace.

"It is so good to have you here again," Mrs. Carrington said. "Your presence brings back sweet memories of all the good times when you and Lucy and Herbert were together." For a moment, she seemed about to weep, but taking a lace handkerchief from her sleeve, she dabbed at her eyes and smiled. "I promise not to mourn, dear child. Herbert is at peace with our Heavenly Father now and will never more know pain and suffering."

Ashlands itself was full of memories, and Elsie seemed to see Herbert everywhere she looked. But Lucy would not allow her to become melancholy. She was too full of her own good news.

"You know that we were in the North this summer," Lucy began as the two girls sat on her bed. "I met someone there, and he is perfectly wonderful! Look!"

She held out her left hand and on the third finger, a beautiful ring of diamonds and rubies glittered in the sunlight.

"You are engaged," Elsie said excitedly. "And your parents approve?"

"Oh, absolutely. He is the son of old friends, but I had never met him before. He is so good and kind and handsome. Very handsome, if I say so myself. You will meet him at Christmas when he comes to visit. We are to be married next June."

They talked for some time about Lucy's engagement, until finally Lucy said, "There now, you have all my secrets. Now you must share yours with me."

After some coaxing — which was Lucy's specialty — Elsie told her about her own summer, about Bromly Edgerton and his proposal, about the sad conclusion.

"I declare, your Papa intends to keep you an old maid for life," Lucy said with just a hint of distaste.

"Oh, no," Elsie protested. "Papa is doing what he thinks best, though I know his judgment of Mr. Edgerton is in error."

"Whatever did the man do to earn your father's displeasure?"

"It was a mistake, but Papa believes him to be a gambler and a forger and a fortune-hunter."

Genuinely shocked, Lucy asked, "On what grounds?"

"Papa has proofs that he thinks convict Mr. Edgerton," Elsie replied. "But Bromly explained it all to me. It is a case of mistaken identity, and Bromly is being blamed for another man's faults. The Bromly Edgerton I know is in every way a gentleman. He even confessed to me that he had been a little wild in his youth, but he has repented and become a true Christian."

"But I suppose you will give him up at your father's command," Lucy said.

"I will never marry without Papa's consent. Though I believe Papa is mistaken, I have no question about his sincere desire to guard me against what he believes to be a grave danger. But it is very confusing, Lucy, and very hard to bear."

Lucy clasped her friend in her arms. "You poor dear," she said softly. "No one deserves her happiness more than you."

The two friends talked frequently of the situation during the next few days. Lucy found no fault with Horace Dinsmore's behavior, yet the more she talked with Elsie, the more Lucy defended Mr. Edgerton. "It's just plain unfair to condemn anyone without a hearing," she frequently declared.

Three days had gone by, and the girls were dressing after an afternoon ride when a servant came to Lucy's room with a message. A gentleman was in the parlor to see Miss Lucy. No, the housemaid did not know the young man. Yes, she would tell him to wait while Miss Lucy finished dressing.

"It's probably a friend of Herbert's," Lucy said. "They still come by, you know, to see that we are well. It's very sweet, but I'm sorry he has chosen an afternoon when my parents and grandparents are out. And I seem to be all thumbs," she added, fiddling at her curls until her complicated hairdo tumbled down from its combs.

"See there! I'll never be ready. Elsie, you are fit to receive a guest. Will you do me a great favor? Go to the parlor and entertain the gentleman until I can pull myself together."

Laughing at her friend's frantic toilette, Elsie agreed. "But hurry along, for I doubt I can keep him entertained for long."

Entering the parlor, Elsie saw a tall man in handsomely tailored attire. His back was to her, and he seemed engrossed in the portrait of Lucy's grandparents that hung above the fireplace mantle. There was something familiar, Elsie sensed, about his stance.

Before Elsie could issue polite greetings, the man turned, came to her, and seized her in his embrace, kissing her hair, her forehead, her cheeks.

"My darling," he sighed, "I have you at last!"

For a few moments, Elsie forgot all else in the warmth of Bromly Edgerton's arms, and she let herself be swept up in his torrent of words and kisses. He loved her, he declared. He had nearly died of longing for her. Her returned letters had broken his heart. He would never do anything to harm her. He had been so cruelly misjudged. Her father was so unfair, so cruel.

Suddenly, Elsie was struggling to free herself.

"This is not right," she cried out. "I must go! Papa has forbidden any contact between us. Oh, what have I done? To allow you to touch me like this. Papa will be so angry."

Bromly had dropped her arms but still clung to her hands. "Then don't go back to him, my angel. I can't bear to see your tears. Come with me. Be my wife, and you shall never again shed a single tear of unhappiness."

"Let me go," she begged. "Please, let me go. I am doing wrong!"

He pulled her close to him again, but she pushed him away. "I'll call for help if you do not loose your grasp, sir,"

she declared, her voice strong, but her body weak and shaking.

He backed away a step. "Don't cry out," he said softly, "for we want no scandal. But my offer stands. Come away with me, Elsie, to a life of joy and happiness."

"Not so long as I am my father's child."

"But when you come of age?"

"I will still be my Papa's daughter, whatever my age."

"And are you prepared to sacrifice your every hope of happiness for him? Will you allow his false prejudice to keep us apart?"

"I *cannot* marry without my father's blessing. Such a union could never be a happy one."

"Then at least hear me out, for I can prove to you now that I am not what your father believes."

Elsie looked into his eyes, and Edgerton read on her face not fear, but eager expectation. He began to talk rapidly, but instead of the proofs Elsie anticipated, he could only pour out more protestations, justifications, and self-serving denials.

After a few minutes of his diatribe, Elsie turned way. "I can hear no more of this," she said tremulously. "I must go." And before he could reach out to grab her again, she ran from the room.

Tears blinding her eyes, she dashed up the stairs, brushing past Lucy. Lucy hurried down and entered the parlor.

Facing Edgerton, she asked "What has happened?"

He began to pace the room, his face livid with his rage and his fists clenched.

"She is a fool!" he exclaimed. "An idiot and a fool! No fortune is worth this!"

"Mr. Edgerton!" Lucy was in shock at the words he had spoken.

Recovering himself instantly, Edgerton became apologetic. "Forgive me, Miss Carrington," he pleaded dolefully. "I'm so upset, I don't know what I'm saying. You must understand, Miss Carrington, how passionate love can get the best of one's tongue."

Lucy held herself rigid and said coldly, "The words you spoke were not those of a man in love. Indeed, they lead me to suspect that Mr. Dinsmore is correct."

Edgerton flushed. "What are you saying, Miss Carrington?"

"That it appears you love her fortune rather than Elsie herself."

"But you are wrong, Miss Carrington," he said in the most heartrending tone he could muster. "I adore Miss Dinsmore and would gladly marry her even if she were penniless. I meant only that her father's guardianship of her fortune is tearing us apart. He seems to see every man as a fortune-hunter."

"Possibly, but I cannot imagine calling my loved one a 'fool' or an 'idiot.'"

"I am almost out of my mind. I hardly know what I'm saying," Edgerton said beseechingly.

"Then your meeting did not go well."

"Not at all, but I am deeply grateful to you that I was able to behold her beauty once again. For a few moments at least, I could look into her face and forget the agonies of the past months. Perhaps you will help me once more. I see now there is only one way that Elsie and I can be together. If I could take her away with me, out of her father's influence, then I know I can persuade her to marry me. Will you help me to take her from here, Miss Carrington? Will you help your friend to escape with me and secure a lifetime of happiness?"

Lucy had been backing toward the parlor door as he spoke. Now she stopped and declared in a voice of ice, "I will never help you with such a scheme, sir. What you propose is kidnapping and worse. I thought only to bring about a reunion, but what you propose is both criminal and dishonorable in every aspect. You must go now, Mr. Edgerton, before I call the servants to remove you."

He started to say something, but Lucy held up her hand and said, "Say nothing. Just go."

Edgerton could see that he had no choice. He hurried from the room and out the front door. Lucy waited until she heard the sound of his horse's hooves galloping down the drive; then she ran upstairs to her friend.

Chloe was packing Elsie's bags, and Elsie was pacing, tears flowing, when Lucy entered the room.

Looking up, Elsie said, "I have no idea why you did this, Lucy, but I must leave immediately. I have disobeyed every one of my father's commands, and I must tell him at once."

Lucy went to Elsie and took her trembling hands. "Oh, dearest friend, I meant you no harm," she said, her own fear and misery cracking her voice. "I wanted only to help you."

At Elsie's incredulous look, Lucy tried to explain. "I met Mr. Edgerton last August when he came to the vacation spot where we were visiting. He seemed such a nice man, and as we conversed, he mentioned that he had been in Lansdale. I asked if by chance he had met you or your Aunt Wealthy, and then his whole story came out. He seemed so bereft at losing you, Elsie, that I believed everything he said. Then he wrote to me after we returned home. He was desperate to know how you were and asked if I could arrange a meeting.

"It seemed so simple when he proposed it. I only thought of your happiness. You must tell your father that it is all my doing and my fault."

Elsie replied more kindly than Lucy had any right to expect, "I am sure you meant well, and I will not blame you for my failings. I should have left that room the instant I saw his face, but I didn't. I broke every promise to my Papa, and now I must tell him."

"Do you have to, Elsie? He need never know."

"I have to," Elsie said firmly. "To withhold the truth would be a deception I couldn't bear. And Papa would immediately see the guilt in my face. I have no secrets from him."

Lucy shook her head sadly. "I know you're doing what's right, Elsie," she said. "I won't try to keep you here. But you must tell your father that this is all my fault."

Elsie put her arm around her friend's shoulder and said gently, "You set things in motion, that's true. But the responsibility is mine."

In sorrow, Lucy left to arrange for one of the stable grooms to accompany Elsie on her ride back to The Oaks and to send a carriage for Chloe and the luggage. She also warned the man, who was one of the most trusted servants at Ashlands, to keep a sharp eye out for anyone who might approach her friend.

Farewells and Homecomings

"There is a man — dark in coloring, about twenty-five or twenty-six years old, and dressed as a fine gentleman — whom I fear may wish Miss Dinsmore harm," she told the groom. "Let him come nowhere near her. You must protect her at all costs and deliver her safely to her father."

CHAPTER 13

A Bitter Pill

"Do not give dogs what is sacred;
do not throw your pearls to pigs.
If you do, they may trample
them under their feet, and
then turn and tear you
to pieces."

MATTHEW 7:6

*R*ose had never seen Horace so angry and depressed. Elsie's return from Ashlands two days early had surprised her parents; her confession had stunned them.

With amazing calm, Elsie told them everything that had happened. She answered every question in detail and took full responsibility for her actions — refusing to assign blame to Lucy or Edgerton. When he had heard her full confession, Horace told her that she would be confined to the house until he allowed otherwise. Then he sent her to her room.

Alone with Rose, he exploded. "Can you imagine it! After all that has happened, she still protects that scoundrel! Lucy Carrington I can understand. She has always been a thoughtless and impulsive girl. But how can Elsie continue to shield that man?"

"I believe she does so because she truly sees herself at fault. Her behavior was not really so terrible in the circumstances, but her obligation to you is the strongest of all her earthly bonds, my dearest," Rose said. "She may yet protect Edgerton out of her innocent sense of fairness, but she loves you, Horace, with all her heart. She is shattered at breaking her promises to you and disobeying your wishes and commands. And she is also suffering because disobeying you is disobedience to the Lord."

"And that is what so enrages me," Horace said, although his anger was losing its strength. "No honest man would set daughter against father as this Edgerton has done. Not once since our meeting on Aunt Wealthy's porch has he attempted to approach me. No, for that is what a man of honor would do, and this scoundrel is dishonorable to his very bones. Truly, dearest, I do not hold Elsie at fault. In fact, I blame myself for not anticipating the tricks of this devil."

"Then perhaps her punishment is a little harsh," Rose said softly. "To be confined to the house and not allowed so much as a walk in the gardens will be very hard on her."

Horace looked at his wife in astonishment. "My order was not intended as punishment," he declared. "Rose, with that man in the neighborhood, I fear for her person. Who knows what he might try next? I don't believe even abduction is beyond him."

A small gasp escaped his wife, and she said, "I had not considered such a possibility, but you're right, Horace. We must protect her by all means."

Horace went to sit beside his wife on the couch. He put his arms around her and drew her close. They sat together in silence, and Horace thought to himself how fortunate he was to have this gentle and wise woman as his beloved companion in suffering as well as joy.

It was ten or fifteen minutes later when Horace finally spoke again. "You've always wanted to see Europe, haven't you?" he asked in an off-hand manner.

Wondering at this strange shift of thought, Rose nevertheless replied simply, "Always, my dear."

"Then I believe the time has come to show you the great capitals: London, Paris, Rome. We might even stop in Edinburgh to visit with our dear old friend Mrs. Murray," Horace proposed. "I think it would require a long trip to see everything — a year at least. I could have my business here tied up in two weeks. And you could take Elsie and

Trip to Philadelphia to await me. I'm sure you can occupy the time productively with shopping and packing for such a long stay abroad."

Rose was smiling now, for she saw the method in her husband's madness.

"It will be good for all of us to get away," she said agreeably. "For Elsie especially. Travel always puts the roses in her cheeks."

"So when might you and the children be ready to go to your parents' home?" he inquired.

"Let's see. This is Tuesday. I believe we can leave on Friday. Will that do, dearest?"

"It will do nicely," he said, pulling her to him for a kiss.

When Horace spoke of his plans to Elsie that night before their prayers, she acquiesced without a murmur. He didn't tell her the fundamental motive for the trip to Europe. She guessed only that he wanted her away from any possible contact with Edgerton, but she never suspected that her parents feared for her safety.

Horace also made his apology for imposing what appeared to be a hard punishment on her, explaining that he asked her to remain in the house to forestall any further difficult situations.

"I understand, dear Daughter, that you were taken by surprise at Ashlands. I don't want you feeling guilty for what you could not have prevented."

"But I didn't run away from Mr. Edgerton, Papa," she said with tears in her eyes. "I should have. I should have obeyed you instantly, without question or hesitation."

Elsie's Stolen Heart

"Elsie, you cannot always do everything right. Remember, there is only One who is perfect. He watches over us in all we do, and He forgives our failures. I have asked Him to forgive me for appearing to punish you harshly when that was not my intention. I don't want any misunderstandings between us, Elsie. I do not blame you, nor even Lucy, for what occurred. And I am proud of you for telling me about it immediately. You didn't have to, you know," he added with a gentle smile.

Elsie's beautiful eyes opened wide. "Oh, Papa, I could never keep anything from you," she said.

"I know you couldn't," he responded, "even when you might have saved yourself some grief."

The next few days flew by in the rush of packing and preparations. Trip was nearly wild with excitement; Rose talked happily of all the things they would do in Europe; and Chloe couldn't help grinning that she was about to see the world. In spite of herself, Elsie was infected by their enthusiasm, and the scene with Edgerton at Ashlands slipped to the back of her mind.

They arrived in Philadelphia on the following Saturday and were immediately swept up in a whirl of activity. The shopping was intensive, and Elsie joked that she saw more of dressmakers than her own family. That was not quite true, for Rose never let the girl out of her sight when they were away from the Allisons' home. As added protection, Horace had sent John with his wife and children, and that valued servant watched over Elsie with the discipline of a soldier guarding the national treasure. Although Elsie was unaware of his precautions, John stayed awake each and every night, watching the townhouse for any sign of an intruder.

A Bitter Pill

On the evening of Horace's arrival two weeks later, Elsie asked if she might accompany John to meet her father at the train station. Assured that John and the carriage driver were alert to any possibility, Rose agreed.

John stayed at Elsie's side on the station platform as Horace's train pulled in, and he followed her every step when she rushed into her Papa's arms. During the carriage ride through the streets of Philadelphia, Elsie chatted for a while, but seeing that the trip had wearied her father, she fell silent and watched out the carriage window.

The darkened streets were relieved at intervals by lamps and the faint glow of lights behind curtained windows, but at one point, the carriage turned a corner, and the night was flooded with bright lights. The carriage slowed almost to a stop.

"What is it, Papa?" Elsie asked, peering out her window at what seemed to be a crowd of people and conveyances parked ahead of them.

"It's a theater, my dear, and it appears that the play has just ended," Horace guessed. "We shall be stuck here for a few minutes, I imagine."

Gazing out, Elsie saw dozens of women and men in fancy dress and heard much laughter and loud conversation. She was enjoying the sight when a familiar voice caught her attention. Her eyes moved across the theatergoers until they stopped on a well-known face, darkly handsome with a sardonic smile. Bromly Edgerton was walking down some steps, and he slipped and staggered. He would have fallen except that he grabbed onto his companion — a woman with unnaturally red hair and wearing feathers and a beaded crimson cape. In the bright lights of the theater, her heavily made-up face appeared hard and garish.

"Watch your step, Tom!" the woman shouted. Then with a raucous laugh, she added, "I bet your little Southern heiress couldn't support you so well."

"Don't talk of her to me," he said in slurred speech. "She can't hold a candle to you, Belle."

"Except for her money," the woman laughed again as they came so close to the carriage that Elsie could have touched them.

"And that's all she ever meant to me," the man sneered, "a pot of gold."

"Tom Jackson, you're a rascal," the woman smirked. "Think you might find a drink for a thirsty friend?"

"Whatever you like, my dear," he said, stumbling forward.

And then they were gone, melting like shadows into the crowd.

Horace put his arm around his daughter, and she slumped against his shoulder. The light revealed her face to be a ghastly pale, and he thought for a moment she might faint. But she clung to him like a drowning person, and he felt shudder after shudder pass through her body. He stroked her brow, and crooned softly, "My poor child. My poor child."

The carriage, freed of the traffic jam, picked up speed, and they were almost at the Allisons' street when Elsie finally spoke.

"How could I have been so blind, Papa? So terribly blind. Thank God for you, Papa. You were saving me all along with your love and protection."

"And thank Him that you are safe with me now, my child."

A Bitter Pill

The truth had been hard for Elsie. For several days, she stayed in her bed, eating nothing and speaking hardly at all. Horace wanted to send for a doctor, but Rose counseled him to wait.

"She is grieving, husband, for a terrible loss," Rose told him.

"Loss? How can you call the truth about that villain a loss?"

"It's not Edgerton — or Jackson as he is — that she mourns, but what he stole from her. He took a piece of her innocence, her child-like trust in the goodness of others. He might have robbed her of her entire fortune and caused her less pain. She needs to grieve for her loss."

"I want to help her," Horace said, his expression clearly showing that his pain was almost as deep as his child's.

"But you have helped and are helping," Rose assured him firmly. "It's your love that saved her and will cure her. You never deserted her, Horace. She will realize that she can trust others because she can trust you. You are her model of an honorable Christian man, while Jackson will become no more than the fading memory of a bad dream. Even so, she will learn a lesson from her experience and be wiser for it. But believe me, darling, she will recover."

"If I could end her pain this instant, I would," Horace said, taking his wife's hands. "But I know One who can. He has already intervened to open Elsie's eyes to the truth. Let's pray to Him now to work His healing power.

Elsie did improve, and several days afterwards, she was feeling well enough for a visitor. Walter had ridden down from his college to see her before the family left for Europe.

They sat together in the parlor, and at first Walter spoke only of his studies and his busy schedule at school.

Then Elsie asked, "How is Arthur?"

"Recovered from his fever, but that's the least of his woes. Papa is furious with him and refuses to send him back to college or to pay his debts. You have no idea how Tom Jackson fleeced him — Arthur owes thousands of dollars, and Jackson had the nerve to write to my father requesting payment of these 'debts of honor.' Papa has turned it all over to Horace."

Elsie, who had blanched at the mention of Tom Jackson, asked, "What does my father plan to do?"

"He will not pay, for he says that there can be no honor in debts to a cheat and a liar. And Papa agrees. I think Horace is very smart in such matters, don't you?"

"I do," she agreed with a little smile.

"Elsie," Walter said hesitantly, "I've been wanting to speak to you about all that's happened. I wanted you to understand about Jackson — "

Elsie turned her head away, and he was afraid she was crying, but he went on anyway. "You aren't the only person he fooled. Until I found that letter to Arthur from Lansdale, I never suspected a thing. I just thought Jackson was another of Arthur's wild friends, but I never even guessed at his true character."

"But you were never so blind as I," Elsie whispered.

"He fooled everyone, Elsie. Let me show you something."

He reached into his pocket and withdrew two letters which he placed side-by-side on the arm of Elsie's chair.

Looking at them quickly, Elsie saw that they appeared to be in the same handwriting.

"Horace received this one" — he pointed to the fresher letter — "just before he left The Oaks. It is from Mrs. Waters, the mother of a friend of mine. She was in Europe all last summer and knew nothing of what was done in her name. Do you see what she writes? 'I have never met anyone named Bromly Edgerton nor written an introduction for him.'

"Now look at this first letter. Aunt Wealthy sent it to Horace to explain how Jackson weaseled his way into her home. See? It's the letter of introduction. It appears to be in Mrs. Waters's writing, and a neater forgery I cannot imagine."

Elsie stared at the two letters for several moments. Then she raised her eyes to Walter and asked, "Why show them to me now? What good will it do when I already know the truth?"

"Horace didn't want you to see them, Elsie. But I think they can help you understand," Walter said. He was forceful and determined, no longer the passive boy Elsie had grown up with. "These letters show that Jackson had concocted his scheme long before he ever laid eyes on you. He cares for no one but himself, and there is nothing you could have done to stop his plan. He lied to everyone from the start, fooling me and Aunt Wealthy and all the people you met in Lansdale and our friend Lucy. If it hadn't been for that chance encounter with Mr. Travilla, no one would have known the truth — not even Horace. Not until it was too late."

Walter leaned forward and continued, "Elsie, I'm sorry for the way I treated you when you lived at Roselands. I always liked you and wanted to stand up for you, but I was so weak and afraid then. I let Arthur and even Enna bully me into keeping quiet all the times when I should have defended you."

Elsie smiled wanly. "I understood that. You've no need to apologize."

"I'm saying this because I don't want you to become weak and afraid now. I don't want Tom Jackson to succeed by making you fearful of others."

He picked up the letters and put them back into his pocket. "I showed you these because you need to know that other good people were deceived by him just as you were. You have nothing to be ashamed of. You must get on with your life and not let your experience make you weak or shake your faith."

Elsie thought over what he had said; then she asked, "How did you know that I would have these feelings, Walter?"

He bowed his head in a shy way that reminded her of the little boy who used to hide behind the door in the playroom.

"Because that is how I always feel when I'm bullied and deceived. I guess I wanted to warn you not to let disappointment and fear take over your life. I want you to go to Europe and feel strong and healthy. I don't want you to jump at shadows or believe in ghosts. Even when you were very little, when you first came to live at Roselands, I could see that you were strong, Elsie. You are even stronger now, and you have Horace and Rose and so many people to love and support you."

"Does that include you, Uncle Walter?" Elsie asked, and he looked up in surprise. There was a happy little tone

in her voice, and her eyes were sparkling. The Elsie he had always known seemed to be emerging from her misery.

"Even me," he replied with a relieved laugh. "If I can turn from meek little Walter into the defender of right and good that you see before you now, then you — Elsie Dinsmore — can survive anything!"

Will Elsie's broken heart be mended?
What surprises await her in Europe?
Will she recognize her true love?

Elsie's story continues in:

ELSIE'S TRUE LOVE

Book Five of the
*A Life of Faith:
Elsie Dinsmore* Series

Available at your local bookstore

A Life of Faith: Elsie Dinsmore Series

* Now Available as a Dramatized Audiobook!

Check out
www.alifeoffaith.com

🌹 Get news about Elsie and her cousin Millie and other *A Life of Faith* characters

🌹 Join the Elsie Club

🌹 Find out more about the 19th Century world Elsie lives in

🌹 Learn to live a life of faith like Elsie

🌹 Learn how Elsie overcomes the difficulties we all face in life

🌹 Find out about *A Life of Faith* products

Collect all of our Millie products!

A Life of Faith: Millie Keith Series

* Now Available as a Dramatized Audiobook!

Collect all of our Violet products!

MCP
Mission City Press

For more information, write to

Mission City Press at 202 Seond Ave. South,
Franklin, Tennessee 37064
or visit our Web Site at:

www.alifeoffaith.com

A LIFE OF FAITH®
Girls Club

An Imaginative New Approach to Faith Education

*I*magine…an easy way to gather the young girls in your community for fun, fellowship, and faith-inspiring lessons that will further their personal relationship with our Lord, Jesus Christ. Now you can, simply by hosting an A Life of Faith Girls Club.

This popular Girls Club was created to teach girls to live a *lifestyle* of faith.

Through the captivating, Christ-centered, historical fiction stories of Elsie Dinsmore, Millie Keith, Violet Travilla, and Laylie Colbert, each Club member will come to understand God's love for her, and will learn how to deal with timeless issues all girls face, such as bearing rejection, resisting temptation, overcoming fear, forgiving when it hurts, standing up for what's right, etc. The fun-filled Club meetings include skits and dramas, application-oriented discussion, themed crafts and snacks, fellowship and prayer. What's more, the Club has everything from official membership cards to a Club Motto and original Theme Song!

For more info about our Girls Clubs, call or log on to:
www.alifeoffaith.com • 1-800-840-2641

— ABOUT THE AUTHOR —

*M*artha Finley was born on April 26, 1828, in Chillicothe, Ohio. Her mother died when Martha was quite young, and James Finley, her father, soon remarried. Martha's stepmother, Mary Finley, was a kind and caring woman who always nurtured Martha's desire to learn and supported her ambition to become a writer.

James Finley, a doctor and devout Christian, moved his family to South Bend, Indiana, in the mid-1830s. It was a large family: Martha had three older sisters and a younger brother who were eventually joined by two half-sisters and a half-brother. The Finleys were of Scotch-Irish heritage, with deep roots in the Presbyterian Church. Martha's grandfather, Samuel Finley, served in the Revolutionary War and the War of 1812 and was a personal friend of President George Washington. A great-uncle, also named Samuel Finley, had served as president of Princeton Theological Seminary in New Jersey.

Martha was well educated for a girl of her times and spent a year at a boarding school in Philadelphia. After her father's death in 1851, she began her teaching career in Indiana. She later lived with an elder sister in New York City, where Martha continued teaching and began writing stories for Sunday school children. She then joined her widowed stepmother in Philadelphia, where her early stories were first published by the Presbyterian Publication Board. She lived and taught for two years at a private academy in Phoenixville, Pennsylvania — until the school was closed in 1860, just before the outbreak of the War Between the States.

About the Author

Determined to become a full-time writer, Martha returned to Philadelphia. Even though she sold several stories (some written under the pen name of "Martha Farquharson"), her first efforts at novel-writing were not successful. But during a period of recuperation from a fall, she crafted the basics of a book that would make her one of the country's best known and most beloved novelists.

Three years after Martha began writing *Elsie Dinsmore*, the story of the lonely little Southern girl was accepted by the New York firm of Dodd Mead. The publishers divided the original manuscript into two complete books; they also honored Martha's request that pansies (flowers, Martha explained, that symbolized "thoughts of you") be printed on the books' covers. Released in 1868, *Elsie Dinsmore* became the publisher's best-selling book that year, launching a series that sold millions of copies at home and abroad.

The Elsie stories eventually expanded to twenty-eight volumes and included the lives of Elsie's children and grandchildren. Miss Finley published her final Elsie novel in 1905. Four years later, she died less than three months before her eighty-second birthday. She is buried in Elkton, Maryland, where she lived for more than thirty years in the house she built with proceeds from her writing career. Her large estate, carefully managed by her youngest brother, Charles, was left to family members and charities.

Martha Finley was a remarkable woman who lived a quiet Christian life; yet through her many writings, she affected the lives of several generations of Americans for the better. She never married, never had children, yet she left behind a unique legacy of faith.